"A thrilling and original adventure"
Guardian

"A pitch-perfect blend of humour, adventure and emotion"
Sunday Telegraph

"Funny, entertaining and surprisingly moving and it is this …
that lifts the book above the ordinary"
Philip Ardagh, *Guardian*

"*Sparks* has a beautiful emotional intelligence and humour that
make its suspense all the more enjoyable. It is one of the best
new books for 9+ out this year"
The Times

"Enterprising writing of a high calibre"
Independent on Sunday

"Proof that magic is really all around us"
Guardian

"Ally Kennen began her writing career well with an acclaimed book
for teens and has gone from strength to strength with each
subsequent novel… Well-observed, witty and moving"
Sunday Times

"Ally Kennen is a wonderful storyteller and she draws the reader in
to this novel with its excellent characterisation and bittersweet plot"
Scotsman

Praise for Ally Kennen

"Inventive, funny and moving family adventure …
one of the season's stand-outs"
Children's Bookseller – Ones to Watch

"Refreshingly different … a well written tale with much wisdom
embedded in the telling. Words that are inspiring, challenging
and encouraging convey the message that the beloved dead
are always with us to inspire, challenge, encourage"
School Librarian

"Rings with talent and compelling detail …
a tense, funny and touching tale"
Amanda Craig, *The Times*

"Ally Kennen is already a remarkably assured writer"
Nicholas Tucker, *Independent*

"An extraordinary imaginative achievement … this is a compassionate
story from an exciting new voice"
Bookseller

ALLY KENNEN grew up on a farm in Exmoor. She is the author of eight novels for children and teens. Her books have been nominated for and won numerous awards.

She lives in Somerset with her husband, three children, chickens, a dog and four and a half cats.

Her ambitions are to write many more books and join a women's football team.

allykennen.blogspot.com

Also by Ally Kennen

HOW TO SPEAK SPOOK (AND STAY ALIVE)
MIDNIGHT PIRATES
SPARKS

Young Adult Titles

BEAST
BEDLAM
BERSERK
QUARRY
BULLET BOYS

Scholastic Children's Books
A division of Scholastic Ltd
Euston House, 24 Eversholt Street
London, NW1 1DB, UK
Registered office: Westfield Road, Southam, Warwickshire, CV47 0RA
SCHOLASTIC and associated logos are trademarks and/
or registered trademarks of Scholastic Inc.

First published in the UK in 2013 by Marion Lloyd Books
This edition published by Scholastic Ltd, 2015

ISBN 978 1407 14559 4

A CIP catalogue record for this book
is available from the British Library

Printed and bound by CPI Group (UK) Ltd, Croydon CR0 4YY
Papers used by Scholastic Children's Books
are made from wood grown in sustainable forests.

This is a work of fiction. Names, characters, places, incidents
and dialogue are products of the author's imagination or are used fictitiously.
Any resemblance to actual people, living or dead, events
or localities is purely coincidental.

For Evie, Angus, Iona and Freya

MIDNIGHT PIRATES

ALLY KENNEN

■SCHOLASTIC

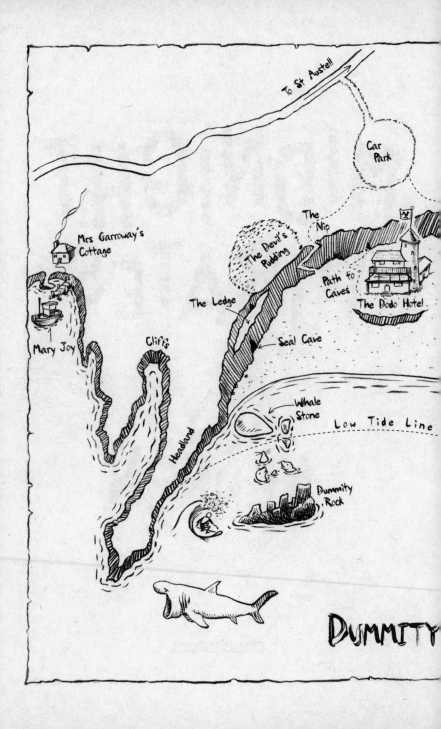

To St Austell

Car Park

The Nip

Mrs Garroway's Cottage

The Devil's Pudding

The Ledge

Path to Caves

The Dodo Hotel

Seal Cave

Mary Joy

Cliffs

Whale Stone

Low Tide Line

Headland

Dummity Rock

DUMMITY

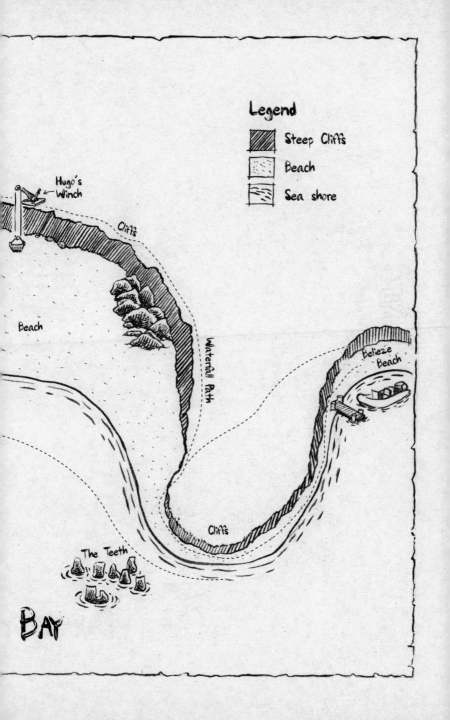

CHAPTER ONE

Miranda Ruins the Mystique

Four mermaids squelched over the damp concrete landing, trying not to trip over their lurid rubber tails. They parked themselves on the edge of the tank. Miranda, the smallest, spat out her chewing gum and stuck it over the leak in her tail. She adjusted her goggles and waited for the show to start. Mrs Reegan, who owned MYRMAID WYRLD, didn't let any of her other employees wear goggles, as she said it "Ruined the Mystique". But because Miranda was a freakishly good swimmer and had waist-length black hair, Mrs Reegan had agreed to let her wear them. Cal, Miranda's sixteen-year-old brother, had said this was the craziest Saturday job he'd ever heard of. It was all right for him, he had seasonal work, helping to teach at the surf school on Fistral Beach. But at only thirteen years old, Miranda had fewer options. Besides, mermaid impersonation was fun, despite the problem of water in her ears from all the underwater somersaults she had to do.

A fat drip of condensation fell from the metal roof, rippling the green-tinged water, which wafted a smell like fermenting marmalade. Miranda peered into the depths of the arena. Ghostly shadows slid beyond the windows below. These were the audience, waiting for their afternoon's entertainment. Miranda tried not to watch as Morag, the chief mermaid, hauled her poison-green tail up and over her vast backside and sucked in her stomach to do up the zip. She started doing some noisy breathing exercises, designed to help her hold her breath for longer.

Miranda never bothered with these. She could hold her breath for four minutes without dying and had the largest lung capacity out of all of the mermaids on every shift.

"How's the Rat Hotel?" Morag panted, catching her eye. Her thick waterproof make-up and her red wig made her look like a bad cartoon.

Miranda stiffened. *Here we go again*, she thought.

"Rats, really?" Patrick, token merman and second in command, was investigating something in his left armpit. "Euuurghh."

"We haven't got rats in our hotel," Miranda protested. She was fairly sure this was true, though there was definitely a mouse or two, or twenty.

"My dad says he's cancelled your meat order because your parents can't pay the bill," breathed Morag, showing chocolate-coated canines. "Sounds like The Dodo Hotel is finally becoming extinct."

"We're doing fine, thank you," snapped Miranda, fighting an urge to push the older girl in the tank. As well as being the chief mermaid, Morag was the butcher's daughter and therefore had access to all sorts of private information.

The red light on the pillar blinked, indicating it was time for the underwater show to begin. Morag slipped a clip on her nose and tossed her fake hair. She cracked her knuckles, slipped off the edge into the arena and vanished, leaving only bubbles popping on the surface. A moment later she reappeared and spat a mouthful of water over Miranda's yellow tail.

"Keep your fins out of my face and don't block my breathing tube this time or your mermaid career is dead." She rolled over, her green bottom wobbling on the surface and her tail thrashing as she dived.

"That was an accident. . ." protested Miranda.

She felt a sympathetic hand on her shoulder. "Don't let Morag gnarl you up, babe." Mermaid three, Doris, was Miranda's brother's girlfriend. She had corkscrew blonde curls. (During the underwater shows the rays found Doris's hair irresistible.)

"She's only jealous because you're the bone-fide mermaid and she's only the Queen of Sausages." Doris indicated the audience below.

"C'mon, it's time to throw some fish shapes."

MYRMAID WRYLD – CORNWALL'S PREMIER AQUATIC ATTRACTION was an aquarium complex situated in a large warehouse on the outskirts of St Austell. As well as the mermaid show in the arena (four times a day in the summer season, six times on Saturdays), there were cabinets and tanks full of neon-lit fish, a cafe with clam cakes and seaweed soup and a gift shop selling bath toys and shell jewellery boxes.

The other main attraction was Clover, a huge, bad-tempered Pacific octopus who had a large tank all to herself. Despite her size she was an accomplished escape artist, delicately compressing and unfurling her watery body to creep through the smallest of holes. She would crawl wetly across the landing and plop into the neighbouring tanks to murder the aquarium's fish. The octopus liked to hide between the rocks, but whenever she caught sight of Miranda she turned bright red with rage, like she knew fried octopus was Miranda's mother's signature dish. Miranda had nightmares about Clover, with her peevish eyes and horrible limbs.

On wet days in the summer, MYRMAID WYRLD was heaving with tourists. Today was sunny, so there were only a few die-hard four-year-olds and their parents.

Miranda tugged at her tail. The chewing gum had come off and water was seeping in, but a little girl was standing, mesmerized, on the other side of the glass. Miranda put her fingers to her mouth, blew out and whipped her air bubbles into the shape of a heart. Turning herself upside down, Miranda put her palm on the glass and the child reached up, her eyes wide. Miranda then swam to the bottom of the tank, had a suck on her breathing tube and batted four tiny green fish out of her face. Above her, the others were wallowing through "The Mer Dance". The three of them started manically twirling, creating a cloud of bubbles which made Miranda want to laugh because it looked like they were doing a massive volley of farts. Miranda wasn't part of the dance. She was officially just a trainee mermaid and she was only really supposed to wave and smile at the audience and deliver the breathing tubes – long hoses through which air was pumped via a nozzle – to the others every two minutes. But Miranda loved to make the audience laugh and stroke the fish and somersault and dance in the water, even though Morag was always telling her to stop showing off.

As Miranda floated up, a tail lashed into her head. Morag violently gestured at her red cheeks. Miranda had forgotten to deliver the breathing tubes. She was not fond of the butcher's daughter but she didn't exactly want to drown her. Miranda dived and plucked the tube from the bottom and swam it up to Morag. The older girl snatched it with such force that Miranda's goggles were knocked askew. She flailed around, seeing nothing but bubbles and her own dark hair. She needed her breathing tube, but where was it? She made out the blurry shapes of the other mermaids dancing the Grand Finale, grabbing each other's tails and swimming in a loop. Miranda's lungs were hurting; she desperately needed to breathe. She looked longingly at the surface. Where was the tube? One of the others must have put it in the wrong place. Miranda could hold her breath for ages and ages but this was longer than she had ever. . .

Miranda felt something cold and slimy on her skin as a streak of orange wrapped tight around her arm. She felt a

5

flood of fear. The octopus! She squealed and lashed out. In the next few seconds, three things happened.

1) She realized it was not Clover wrapping her tentacles round her but Morag's red wig.
2) In a moment of mad wickedness, which she would later blame on oxygen starvation, Miranda found herself yanking the red wig off the older girl's head.
3) Her tail, now heavy with water, slipped down over her legs and circled to the bottom of the tank, revealing Miranda's yellow-skull shorts and knobbly knees.

Choking and coughing, Miranda broke the surface, leaving her tail rolling on the bottom of the tank like a cast-off skin.

"YOU'RE FIRED." The words swam into her drenched ears.

CHAPTER TWO

The Dodo Hotel

The bus laboured up the cliff road, blowing out black smoke and rattling like an earthquake. Miranda watched a black-winged jackdaw swoop over the sea. One day she would fly up this hill in a silver Mercedes, zipping past caravans and lost tourists, the engine purring like a fat tiger.

A dribble of aquarium water ran from her hair down her neck. Pulling Morag's wig off, even though she deserved it, was a bad thing to do. And the worst crime at MYRMAID WYRLD was to give away that they weren't real mermaids (even though everyone over the age of three knew the truth).

"YOU HAVE DESTROYED THE MYSTIQUE," Mrs Reegan had hissed in the damp changing room, her nostrils widening so much that Miranda could see the hairs inside.

"It will be all over YouTube." Morag had raked her

hand through her real, spiky, green hair. "This will ruin my career." She'd lurched towards Miranda in her tail, her clawed hand raised ready to strike.

"C'mon, Morag, mermaid queens don't attack li'l girls." Doris caught Morag's arm. And Miranda turned and ran out through the gift shop and into the car park in her flip-flops and wet shorts.

She'd worked at MYRMAID WYRLD since April; that was five months. She liked the work and loved the wages, but being a mermaid had also earned her respect at school. None of her friends lived in ancient beach hotels. Most of them inhabited warm, normal houses in St Austell, with flat walls, a square of grass out the back, and plenty of hot water. Their parents had names like "Linda" and "Rich". Miranda's parents were called Cormac and Pinkie-Sue MacNamara. Other girls arrived at school with polished fashionable shoes and smelling of hair mousse. Miranda would turn up with tufts of seaweed in her shoes, sand in her hair and smelling of the fried breakfasts they served to the guests. But when she'd got the job as "Little Myrmaid" everyone had been intrigued.

So Miranda stuck at the job and every week she put her wages in her bank account. She was saving up for a car. She knew roughly what she wanted, a nice little diesel hatchback, a starter car which wouldn't lose too much value when she later traded it in for something more powerful. She liked French cars but she was prepared to look at Japanese makes too. She'd be seventeen in three and a half years and by then she ought to have enough money to buy some decent wheels. But now she'd have to find another Saturday job.

Miranda extracted *GLITZ*, a teen magazine, out of her bag. She'd found it at the bus stop. She skipped through until she reached the problem page. Reading about other people's difficulties should make her feel better.

Dear Cas,

I wish I was more normal. Nobody likes the things I like. . .

"HA," said Miranda. It could have been written by her. The group of girls she hung out with at school were obsessed with Ralphie Dvee, a Canadian pop star. If Miranda talked about her stuff, like the ghosthunters who came to stay at the hotel, or the time her younger brother, Jackie, tried to buy an ex-army tank using her parents' eBay account, no one was interested.

Miranda moved on to the next problem.

Dear Cas,

What is going on? I am officially now a teenager but I still haven't got any boobs.

What was this? A conspiracy? It was like the page had been tailor-made for her. She moved swiftly on.

Dear Cas,

My dad seems really sad these days. I can't remember the last time I heard him laugh.

Miranda screwed up the magazine and shoved it in her bag. This stuff wasn't distracting. It was goading her. She brought out *Autotrader* instead. She smiled as she leaned back and leafed through the adverts for second-hand cars of every colour and description. This was more like it.

After Miranda got off the bus she had to walk another

9

half a mile up a steep, narrow lane until she reached the small car park on the cliff. There was nothing else here but the scrubby headland. The nearest dwelling was a cottage about a quarter of a mile further along the coast where old Mrs Garroway, the gardener, lived. Miranda looked out across the bay. The tide was out and Dummity Beach was dotted with shells and seaweed before it steeply shelved to the water. The rock pools below the far cliffs glimmered in the evening sunshine. And there, nestled pinkly below, was The Dodo Hotel. It was about three hundred years old. It sat on a rocky shelf only a few metres above the beach and was a long, L-shaped building with slate roofs and thick stone walls. Over the centuries, new bits had been added, but most striking was The Circus, a fat tower that rose thirty feet out of the eastern elevations. A flag depicting a sprightly dodo fluttered from the parapet. On fine mornings Pinkie-Sue would serve the more intrepid guests their breakfasts up there. The Circus had been built by "Victorian Hugo", a nutty old man who had lived alone at The Dodo for over sixty years in the 1800s. It was rumoured he still haunted the place, and The Dodo Hotel had a half-page write-up in *The Ghosthunter's Guide To The British Isles,* though Miranda tried not to believe in ghosts. She and her two brothers had been born there and as far as she was concerned that gave her more rights to the place than any mouldering old spirit. Sometimes she thought of The Dodo as a kind of third parent. Cormac and Pinkie-Sue were always busy doing the million jobs which needed to be done to run a hotel. They were distracted by guests and bills and staff and deliveries and inspectors. But The Dodo Hotel, with its network of landings and corridors, solid and old, always felt safe. Miranda could see her mother now, a small figure in her yellow sari top and jeans, shaking out the mats in the back garden, causing a flurry of gulls to descend hopefully towards her.

Miranda looked out to sea, trying to find movement within the water. And sure enough, in the sheltered pools that brimmed within a swirl of rocks she saw long, slim shadows, bobbing and flickering in the light.

Pushing through bracken and seagrass, Miranda followed the rocky steep path, known as The Nip, down to the beach. Guests had to leave their vehicles in the car park at the top of the cliff. Cormac said The Nip was a "Unique Selling Point", but Miranda suspected it was why the hotel was never very busy, even in the high season.

When she reached the broad flat rock at the bottom of The Nip, Miranda dumped her bag, kicked off her shoes and jumped off the ledge straight on to the beach. Her body board and fins were lying where she'd left them, under a crusty lobster pot. Tucking them under her arm, she waded over the narrow river that streamed from the base of the cliff into the sea and ran down the beach to where her other family was waiting.

CHAPTER THREE

Dummity Bay

The baby was asleep, floating on its back in the water, eyes closed, its little body rising and falling with the rhythm of the sea. Miranda was so close she could touch it. She looked round for the mother but the baby seemed to be alone. Treading water, Miranda held out her hand, and stroked the soft white-and-grey-speckled body. She felt a thrill like an electric shock run up her arm and watched as the baby gently paddled the water. It grunted and woke, staring at her with startled black eyes.

"Hello, Mica."

The baby hesitated, then whipped itself away, gliding into the depths.

Unable to believe her luck, Miranda swam towards the Dummity Rock, an oddly shaped outcrop that now, at low tide, jutted high out of the water like giants' fingers. Miranda gripped the rough rock and climbed out. She sat dangling her legs in the clear water and wondering if Mica would come back. More likely she was headed for the rocks below the headland where she had been born. Miranda felt jittery with excitement. She didn't know anyone who had stroked a baby seal.

The pup was four weeks old. There had been another but Miranda hadn't seen it for ages and she had come to the sad conclusion that it had died in the late-summer storm a fortnight ago. Mica was now very fat and her mother, Alice, was getting less and less inclined to look after her. Soon she would abandon the baby altogether. Baby seals had to fend for themselves from a very young age and many of them didn't make it.

A brown, sleek head with a distinctive black horseshoe of spots popped out of the water twenty feet away. Sparkling eyes regarded her, then slid beneath the surface. Miranda waited. Two seconds later, the seal reappeared, a little closer.

"Hello, Pasty," said Miranda. This seal had been rescued from a fishing net three years ago and had been released back into the wild. She hadn't yet managed to have any pups.

A second, smaller head appeared and watched her.

"Hello again, Mica," whispered Miranda. She sat as still as she could, watching the seals watching her. An eerie cry broke the quiet, then another, wails that rose and fell, the noise coming from the base of the headland cliffs, where the deep water broke over the rocks. Miranda watched two more seals, one grey, the other large and dark, as they sang, basking in the heat reflected from the stones. She had named the elderly grey one Grandma, and the large dark male Hugo, after the Victorian hermit who had built the Circus tower.

Mica coughed as she bobbed in the water.

"You've got to learn to catch fish for yourself now," Miranda told her sternly.

Mica twitched her whiskers and slipped off.

Out to sea, a red shape rose and fell with the incoming waves. Cal, Miranda's older brother, was out in the deep water. Miranda dropped back into the sea on her board and kicked out to meet him.

Miranda's friends said Cal was very good looking, with his big brown eyes and his wide, relaxed face. And all the children had inherited their mother's brown skin and thick black hair.

"Hey, babe." Cal beamed at his sister. "I just had this backside goofyfoot thing going on. It was sick!" He had a slow Californian drawl, even though Pinkie-Sue was half Mauritian, Cormac was Irish, and Cal had lived in Cornwall all his life.

"I just stroked a baby seal," said Miranda, shifting her weight on her board. "It was asleep in the water."

"That's uber, babe." Cal looked concerned. "But don't go getting attached. Nature is way crueller than us. Seal pups are fluffy bundles of untimely death."

Miranda knew her brother was right.

"Most of them starve," said Cal, sucking in his cheeks to

illustrate the point.

"OK," replied Miranda.

"Or wipe out on the rocks. . ."

"I got fired," Miranda announced to stop him.

"Dude, it was only a matter of time. You were like a rogue mermaid. What did you do?" asked Cal.

"Forgot the breathing tubes, pulled Morag's wig off in the Grand Finale, lost my tail and Ruined the Mystique."

Cal frowned. "You didn't forget Doris's tube?"

"Course not," said Miranda hurriedly.

Cal nodded, relieved. He pointed to the shore. "Look, there go those wild party beasts."

A group of elderly people were scrambling up The Nip. These were the last of the summer guests, twenty members of the Ghosthunter's Society, who had stayed at the hotel for one week hoping to catch sight of Hugo. They'd been a cheery, uncomplaining bunch, even the ones with steel hips and walking sticks. They joked that they would have to be taken up the cliff on the winch. This was a huge metal pulley which had been set into the cliff one hundred and fifty years ago by Hugo, to transport building materials down the cliff. Pinkie-Sue and Cormac had adapted it for luggage, food deliveries and the laundry.

"They're totally cranked up because apparently Hugo showed up last night," said Cal.

"Don't talk about it," shivered Miranda.

She spotted her dad giving a piggyback to a round old lady. As ever, Cormac was immaculately dressed in his tweed suit and checked shirt. He never wore jeans like other dads. Someone had given him some for Christmas, and he'd looked like a sinister hitch-hiker in them.

"I should go and help," said Cal, steering his board round. "Or that senior chick will give the headman serious heart issues. He's struggling."

"At least he's out there and not locked away in his office," said Miranda. She started to head to the shore.

"Don't forget The Burning," Cal called after her.

The Burning was a beach party the family held every year to mark the end of the summer season. It was usually good fun but this year lots of people said they couldn't come.

Five minutes later Miranda climbed the broad stone steps of her home. She opened the black, studded front door and walked into the reception, her bare feet sinking into the soft red carpet. She replaced a spade which had fallen out of a container of beach toys (for the use of the younger guests) and threw a chewed bone, presumably belonging to Fester, their dog, into the wastepaper basket. She picked up a leaflet lying in the fireplace. It was the brochure Cormac had made to advertise the hotel.

The Dodo Hotel – Cornwall's Best Kept Secret

The secret, Miranda mused, had been so well kept that nobody knew they were here. Ghosthunters aside, they simply couldn't attract enough guests.

She stooped to restack an entire shelf of books which must have been pulled out by somebody (not Hugo) and now lay higgledy-piggledy all over the floor. The books belonged to her father and cases lined the walls in the restaurant, the bar, the sitting room and in the family's private living rooms. Cormac was obsessed with books and couldn't stop collecting them. He'd also been writing one for as long as Miranda could remember. It was about hermits, and Victorian Hugo had his very own chapter. The most haunted part of The Dodo was supposed to be The Circus, where Hugo was said to patrol at night.

Miranda eyed a black and white photograph above the reception desk. The copperplate caption read

MR HUGO OATIS

He was a huge, broad man, over six feet tall, with weightlifter's shoulders, a curling moustache, bushy sideburns and a dark, ill-fitting suit. He'd been photographed on the parapet of The Circus, arms folded, with a large smooth-haired dog sitting smartly next to him. He was looking right at the camera and the whites of his eyes looked too bright against the rest of the photograph, giving him a creepy look. It was also said that in times of great danger, Hugo would walk the cliffs on the headland. Miranda pulled her towel tighter round her and punched open the damp window in the tiny office behind the reception desk.

Cormac spent most of his time here, but now there was only the teetering stack of his manuscript, a larger stack of unopened bills, a sleeping computer and a curling pickle sandwich.

"Darling, don't open that window, the gull gets in and poos everywhere," said a low, anxious voice.

Miranda's mother was standing in the doorway leading

to the back hall, her arms full of the ghosthunters' sheets. She was only an inch taller than her daughter and had her glossy black hair cut into a short bob.

"You're back early," noted Pinkie-Sue.

"I got fired," said Miranda.

Pinkie-Sue dumped the washing on the floor and came to give her daughter a hug. She smelled, as she always did, of lilies. "Poor thing," she said, stroking her daughter's wet hair. "What did you do?"

Miranda noted that both her mother and her brother immediately assumed that it was she, Miranda, who had Done Something to merit being fired, rather than being the victim of an injustice.

She told Pinkie-Sue about Morag.

"You could have drowned," said Pinkie-Sue. She gave a little growl. "That horrendous woman, Mrs Reegan, ugh!"

"She paid well," said Miranda. "Unlike here."

Pinkie-Sue released her and straightened her clothes.

"That's true," she said sadly, and picked up the washing. She made for the door leading to the back hallway.

"Don't forget. . ."

"The Burning," supplied Miranda, feeling bad that she had upset her mother.

Pinkie-Sue hesitated. "Darling," she began, "about tonight. . ."

"Yes?" Miranda waited, expecting a list of instructions. "Are we going to sacrifice Fester to the God of Tourism, to reverse our fortunes?"

But Pinkie-Sue didn't smile. Instead she fiddled with the

washing. "I just had to say. About your dad, well. He really needs a holiday and. . . Oh, what's that?"

A loud crash had come from the kitchen.

"They're so busy in there, I better go. . ." Pinkie-Sue made for the door.

Miranda tutted. "Looks like you bottled out on something there, Mumma."

"I did," agreed Pinkie-Sue, but she left the room anyway. The door swished shut.

Miranda frowned. She looked at Hugo.

"Can you tell me what's going on?" she asked the stern photograph. The wind lifted the curtain and slapped it against the glass and Miranda decided to go upstairs and change.

There really was no such thing as ghosts.

CHAPTER FOUR

The Burning

Two hours later Miranda stepped down on to the beach. She wore her favourite green dress and black hoody and was carrying a tray full of glasses. A bonfire blazed and smoke drifted over the sand.

"Hola, hermana!" cried a voice nearby. "Watch it."

The voice came from a large hole dug where the pebbles met the sand. Jackie and Fester stuck their heads out. Jackie was small and sturdy with too much hair. At ten years old, he liked spying, singing and his dog, Fester. He disliked school and underpants. "He needs a little polish," Pinkie-Sue said. "But he's not so different from your father before I married him."

Miranda halted. The sides of the hole were shored up with bits of broken surfboard.

"What's this?"

"I'm not feeling sociable," said Jackie. "Please go away."

Fester scrabbled out of the hole to greet her. He had wandered into the bar of The Dodo Hotel eight years previously and had never left. His parentage was the source of many debates, as he had the long flexible spine of a greyhound, the low-slung belly of a pregnant Labrador, and the feathery tail of a pampered collie. Fester's eyes were the colour of an amber traffic light. He had fat paws and a single fang protruded from his overshot jaw. Fester was no beauty, but he had charm. He adored cats and rabbits but despised team sports. He had many love affairs with the visitors' dogs, causing Pinkie-Sue and Cormac great embarrassment. Though he worshipped Cal (everyone loved Cal), his favourite companion was Jackie, and the two were rarely apart.

"Looks like there's a storm coming," said Miranda, trying to be friendly.

This was a family joke. Guests loved storms. It was one of the things they wanted. They required 1) sand 2) sea 3) sun 4) nice food with chips 5) very clean sheets indeed 6) ghosts 7) a storm on the last night, with lightning and a boiling black sea, with waves smashing into the cliffs with a booty of dead fish and a tangle of sea rope on the chilly shingle the next morning.

"This is a day of doom," said Jackie. "My reconnaissance has discovered that our parents are liars and traitors and life as we know it is about to end." He eyed his sister. "I will make a heroic gesture. I will go out in a blaze of glory."

"Do you want onions on your hot dog?" asked Miranda absently.

"Yes, please," said Jackie.

Miranda wandered on down the beach, towards the gathering party. She counted nine people so far, made up of locals, staff and friends. Trestle tables were loaded with tomato salad, cold roast beef, goat's cheeses, guacamole and breads and crisps and anything else that had been left in the hotel fridges.

Miranda put down her tray and waved at Doris. As well as mermaiding, Cal's girlfriend worked part-time as a waitress at the hotel.

Cormac was poking the barely smoking barbecue. It was made from a cut-in-half oil drum that had once washed up on the beach. The meat on the grill was still pink and raw. Cormac had thick brown hair and skin so white you could see the blue veins in his wrists and his temples.

"Miranda!" he called, spotting his daughter. "Why aren't you helping?"

Miranda frowned. Cormac was so bad-tempered these days.

"I've been working."

"Haven't you resigned from that awful exploitative job yet?" Pinkie-Sue obviously hadn't told him Miranda's news.

"They pay better wages than you." Miranda fixed her father with a challenging glare.

"What sort of people pay to see young women dressed up, masquerading as mermaids?" huffed Cormac.

"It's just underwater dancing," said Miranda. "With a

22

tail." She chased the napkins that had blown off the table. She didn't want to tell him she'd been fired. He would be delighted and that would be annoying.

Cormac knelt to blow on the smouldering charcoal. "It's sinister, demeaning and distasteful."

"You're so grumpy," said Miranda. "It's The Burning. We're supposed to be having fun."

"Howzit beach crew."

Everyone turned to watch as Cal paddled in from the sea, water glistening on his brown shoulders as he pulled down the top of his wetsuit.

"Hey, grey-belly," he grinned at his father. "Did you see that kick-out? Like smooth?"

"You're hardly dressed for dinner," muttered Cormac. Cal's damp ponytail hung over his shoulder.

"Got my boardies behind the rock, I'll be trussed up before the big show." He spotted Doris, laying out plates. "Hey, sick girl!"

"Hey yourself, bruddah, I clocked that brain freeze," called back Doris.

"Romance is not dead," muttered Cormac. "Ouch." He whipped his hand away from the barbecue and sucked his finger. Cal then took a packet of firelighters from a bag under the table and placed them in the oil drum. He held out his hand for Cormac's matches and had a blaze going in minutes.

"You going to sing for us tonight, dude?" Cal picked some ash from his father's hair. Traditionally at The Burning, when it got late, Cormac would bring out his ukulele and launch into a medley of Irish folk songs. He had a deep, gentle singing voice that would get more and more powerful as the night wore on.

"Maybe not this year," Cormac smiled humourlessly. "Only the young should sing of love."

"That's like, morose," said Cal. He started to say more but a nudge from Miranda stopped him. He caught sight of a large raw fish lying on a tray.

"Woo, what a beauty. This has to have come from your line, Mrs G?"

Mrs Garroway, who looked after the garden, was standing a little way off, jabbing a chair leg into the bonfire. She wore a green headscarf, navy trousers and a man's blue shirt. There was a big smudge of charcoal on her wrinkly old cheek. No one knew exactly how old she was, but the current opinion was that she was in her late seventies.

"And *pympes* more," she said nonchalantly.

"Five fish! You are truly a Goddess of the Sea, Mrs G," said Cal. He took a knife, slit the fish and expertly gutted it.

"You won't catch me with your silver tongue, princeling." Mrs Garroway was scowling at Cal but everyone knew the old woman had a soft spot for him.

"*Deeth da*, Mrs G," called Miranda.

At the sound of the Cornish words, Mrs Garroway's old face cracked into a smile. "*Darzona*, maid," she called back, the chair leg smouldering in her hand.

The hotel garden stretched round the sides and back of the building and was rammed with sea holly and salt-tolerant roses.

24

Mrs Garroway was particularly proud of her gorse topiary sharks round the patio picnic tables and was forever pruning a fin here or sharpening a tooth there. Her natural facial expression was one of mild irritation. When she was young she had worked in various harbours around the country as a pilot, guiding large ships into port. Now she lived in her tiny tin-worker's cottage on the headland. The council were trying to persuade her to move as the cliff was gradually eroding and in a few years it would not be safe. But Mrs Garroway would not budge. No-nonsense, deeply practical, and sharp-tongued as she was, most people were a little bit afraid of her. She always did exactly as she liked and didn't care what people, or the law, thought of her.

"And here I am," sang Pinkie-Sue as she sailed over the sand, bearing a steaming dish of rice. Miranda scrutinized her mother. She was wearing her long red battle dress, the outfit she wore when she needed to have courage. It was usually brought out for meetings with the bank manager or at Jackie's school's parents' evenings. Pinkie-Sue was also wearing all her silver bracelets, she'd swept her hair into an updo and she'd applied glittery green eyeshadow.

Miranda felt uneasy and detached but couldn't think why. She leaned into the Whale Stone, a lone granite outcrop near the high-tide line and watched as Toby the chef, Una the head waitress and Polly and Jane, the summer girls, arrived. Behind them were a crowd of locals and the unmistakable figure of Great Aunty Mad, Cormac's mother's sister, who was wearing a large red rain hat despite the evening sun.

At first everything seemed to go right. The sun shone on their corner of the beach, the bonfire blazed with old furniture and Cal's exam revision, and the meat, when it was ready, was perfectly edible. Mrs Garroway stood by the bonfire, eyes shut, enjoying the heat. Una checked her BlackBerry for messages (there was no mobile signal down here but she never stopped trying) and Toby was chatting to Cal and Doris about a surf competition in Newquay. Aunty Mad touched Miranda's shoulder. She was a pale, thin woman with a pointy chin and a spray of grey-brown hair over her collar.

"He's bearing up," she whispered, nodding at Cormac. "What do you think of the news?" She forked in a mouthful of rice.

"What news?" asked Miranda.

Mad coughed out grains of rice. "They haven't told you yet?"

But just then Cormac stood and moved to be beside his wife and everyone fell silent.

"Welcome to The Burning," he said. Pinkie-Sue squeezed his arm.

"For those of you who don't know," he went on, "we revived the custom of The Burning twenty years ago, when Pinkie-Sue and I fell in love with this place."

"Love is blind," muttered Pinkie-Sue.

"Hugo Oatis, who rebuilt The Dodo in 1869, lived alone, writing his philosophies and poems. But on this day, the first weekend in September, he built a mighty bonfire, invited his neighbours and burned his year's work. It was an act, he wrote, to symbolize the futility of utility. . ."

26

"Are there any more sausages?" interrupted Jackie. "Fester is starving."

Cormac went on. "To cut a long story short. . ."

"Not his greatest talent," Mad whispered to Miranda.

"We now use the occasion to get rid of old ties. . ."

"Letters from the bank manager," said Pinkie-Sue darkly.

"And to thank you all for your hard work and dedicated loyalty. . ."

"For accepting the minimum wage," mumbled Pinkie-Sue.

Miranda watched her father. He was looking odd, if not ill. His pale skin was flushed and he had deep rings under his eyes. Normally he would be cracking jokes and even reading bits out of his book. Today he just seemed to want to get the speech over as quickly as possible.

"Thank you all so very. . ."

Cormac stopped talking and looked at the ground.

"I can't keep up the deceit," he told Pinkie-Sue.

"It's all right," said Pinkie-Sue quietly. "You're doing fine."

Everything seemed to go very quiet.

Cal stood. "Guys, if you're gonna have a wrestle, I'll be the ref. No dirty fighting, no biting or spitting."

Nobody laughed.

Cormac's gaze rested on Miranda. He gave her a look of such sadness that Miranda felt her pulse begin to race. Why was Dad being so weird?

"We have three bits of news," said Cormac.

"Not now, we agreed, not now." Pinkie-Sue shook her

head and blew out her cheeks. She looked at Miranda and bit her lip.

Everybody else pretended to be very interested in their food or looking at the sea.

Cormac cleared his throat again.

"I have a publisher who wants to buy the book. He's based in the States and he wants me to fly out there and meet lots of people."

There was a relieved pause, then someone started clapping, then everyone was clapping and cheering and whooping. Cormac looked pleased and a bit shy. Cal and Doris seized the opportunity to kiss each other. Miranda ran over and hugged her father.

"Well done, Pa," she said. She knew how much this must mean to him. Cormac had been writing his hermit book for years.

"This chap wants me there for a week."

"At last," murmured Mrs Garroway.

"Are we going to be rich?" asked Miranda hopefully.

All the twinkle went out of Cormac's eyes. "It's not that sort of book, I'm afraid."

Cal clapped his father on the back. "None of us thought you had it in you."

"So what is the second piece of news?" asked Miranda.

Cormac swallowed. "It might be a bit of a shock. . ."

"They'll be in therapy for years after this," snapped Pinkie-Sue, putting an arm round her daughter.

"Pinkie's cousin is getting married in October and we haven't been over to Mauritius for years. . ."

"So we're going to the island in the sun!" yelled Jackie, and thumped the table.

"Granny Lamarque is paying for Cormac and I to go with her," said Pinkie firmly. "I'm afraid it's too complicated to take everyone. We'll fly straight from America and we'll be gone for nearly eight weeks." She gave Miranda a hug and whispered in her ear. "Daddy *really* needs this break, darling. I'm so worried about him."

Miranda swallowed. Why were they saying this in front of everyone? This was family stuff.

"You should have talked to us about it first," she snapped, tears welling up.

"I know," Pinkie-Sue agreed. "But we weren't sure it would happen. We didn't want to worry you unnecessarily. . ."

Miranda pushed her mother away and walked a little way off. Eight weeks was *ages*. "How are we supposed to manage without you?"

Pinkie looked sorrowful. "That's the third thing."

"Oh dear," said Miranda's father, and coughed again. "I'm afraid Pinkie-Sue and I have some very big news." He put his palms on the table and gazed into his plate of spare ribs and salad. "Very big."

"You're not having another baby?" yelped Jackie in alarm. He looked wild-eyed at Pinkie-Sue. "I thought you looked a bit fat."

Cormac looked round at everyone. "Oh dear," he said.

"It's all right," repeated Pinkie-Sue. "Your timing is awful but it will be OK."

Miranda felt a surge of irritation. She wished her father

29

would stop fudging and get on with it. Fester put his head in her hand and drooled on her dress and she pushed him away.

"We are selling The Dodo," said Cormac.

A collective gasp was swept away on the breeze. Miranda didn't think she had heard correctly.

"What did you just say?"

"We're selling The Dodo," Cormac repeated quietly.

Had he gone mad? Miranda looked at her mother for reassurance but none came. Pinkie-Sue was now holding Cormac's arm, like she was keeping him upright.

This was impossible. The Dodo was their home, their life, their everything.

Still not able to take it in, Miranda watched the staff sitting with sadly knowing faces, saw her mother fighting back the tears, saw Cal and Doris embracing in commiseration. But then a small boy bomb overturned his chair and knocked his plate to the floor. Jackie flew up the beach, closely followed by Fester.

"Ha ha, very funny," said Miranda. "Awful joke, Dad." She felt someone take her hand. Aunty Mad stood grim-faced next to her.

"I wish I was joking," said Cormac. "And I'm deeply sorry. We aren't making any money. We haven't done for years."

The hotel staff nodded like they already knew.

Cormac tried to smile but didn't quite manage. "Everyone warned us not to rename the hotel 'The Dodo'."

Miranda wiped away the tears that were suddenly flowing over her face.

"We can work this out," she said fiercely. "How can we possibly sell up? I can't leave the seals. Mica needs me."

"Miranda, listen," Aunty Mad was whispering in her ear. "There's more to this than you realize. Your father. . ."

"YES, YES, HE NEEDS A BREAK," snapped Miranda.

Cormac shook his head sadly. "I'm sorry." He wiped his head with his handkerchief and gazed round at his staff. "Please feel free to ask me questions, but the bottom line is, we're broke." He paused. "And I'm broken."

Suddenly Pinkie-Sue screamed. "Call the fire brigade, somebody. Jackie's climbing the cliff!"

CHAPTER FIVE

Goodbyes

Miranda paused in the doorway of her bedroom. It was a circular room beneath the parapet of The Circus. Sometimes, when she was supposed to be in bed, Miranda would tiptoe up to The Circus and sit on the ledge in the darkness and watch the grey sea. Once or twice she'd thought she had seen something flicker in the corner of her eye, or a shadow she couldn't pinpoint, but mostly it was just a peaceful place.

All three children were being sent to a boarding school in North Devon (paid for by their Aunty Mad, who used to teach science there) whilst their parents were away.

"It's difficult for you, I know, but it will only be for a term," Pinkie-Sue had said. "Then we'll get a new house and we'll all be together again."

Miranda thought back to the night of The Burning. Jackie was still in disgrace, as a Coastguard rescue team, an ambulance and a fire engine were deployed to rescue him when he wedged himself in a crevice halfway up the cliff, and even then he had thrown his pants at the man who had abseiled down to collect him. He had only agreed to move after Cormac, shouting through the megaphone Pinkie-Sue used to call Cal in from the sea, had threatened to take Fester to the RSPCA.

After everyone had calmed down, the children had learned the following things.

1) They were to move out in three weeks.
2) The Dodo Hotel would be put on the market immediately and the staff would be laid off.
3) Great Aunty Mad would look after Fester.

"How will I surf?" asked Cal in a voice Miranda had never heard before. Pinkie-Sue stood up and put her arms round her tall son.

"Aunty will take you out at weekends."

"Only at weekends?" Cal's voice was incredulous. "I'm taking all my boards," he said, uncharacteristically fierce.

"I don't know that there will be room at the school to take *all* your boards," she said gently. Cal had fifteen.

"Mica's mother has abandoned her," said Miranda. "She might need extra fish. She might starve."

"I'm sorry," said Pinkie-Sue. "I wish we could stay."

"Why can't we come with you and Granny Lamarque

to America and Mauritius? I want to go to the wedding," stormed Jackie.

"Granny can only pay for the three of us to go," said Pinkie-Sue. "But we've got the internet, and I promise it really won't be for long."

Now Miranda stared through the salt-licked window at the sea. The morning sunlight was dancing on the water and she could see Mrs Garroway out fishing in her little boat, *Mary Joy*.

Later tonight, Cormac and Pinkie-Sue were meeting up with Pinkie-Sue's mother, Granny Lamarque, who lived in London, and flying to America. They were leaving all the big furniture behind so the place "looked more attractive to buyers". And now the guest-room beds were draped in white sheets, the bar area was covered in brown paper and the house sounded different, as all of Cormac's books, papers and knick-knacks had been loaded into crates, winched up the cliff, and taken off to storage or dumped in the outhouse until they could be collected.

They'd said goodbye to the staff last week with hugs and tears.

Miranda heard footsteps on the landing and knew it was her mother.

Pinkie-Sue stepped into the room. She looked very tired and she was wearing her red battle dress.

"You've got about ten minutes," said Pinkie-Sue miserably. "I wish this had turned out differently, but Dad is so excited about his book, and the holiday." Her voice wobbled. "Hopefully he'll come back a happier, healthier man." She kissed her daughter's neck and crept away.

Miranda watched her seals bob in the water for the last time. Mica was rapidly losing weight as she learned to catch her own food. The next few weeks would be make or break for her. Miranda had crept out last night in the moonlight, waded into the dark water and called goodbye to each seal, one by one.

Goodbye, Mica. Goodbye.

It was actually happening! They were walking up The Nip for the last time. Cormac and Cal had already hoisted the bags up the cliff on Hugo's winch. The beach looked the same: wheeling seabirds, pounding waves; the Dummity Rock was being washed by the incoming tide. A glossy head, maybe Pasty, peeped from the water. Miranda walked up The Nip, following Cal. She couldn't believe this was real. All the ground-floor windows of the hotel had been boarded up and a tall metal fence enclosed the garden. A big FOR SALE sign wobbled in the wind.

They'd left The Dodo for ever.

The next day the children found themselves squeezed on to a bus. They'd spent the night on the floor in Aunty Mad's cramped flat. Aunty Mad was a retired scientist. She spent most of her time campaigning for or against things and her flat was packed with leaflets and letters from MPs and political newsletters. She was currently campaigning about wind farms (Miranda could never quite work out if Aunty Mad was for or against them) and nuclear power stations (ditto). Whenever Miranda had asked Aunty to explain, she'd received such long-winded answers that she'd lost track. Aunty Mad owned a small yellow Mini, but rarely drove it anywhere, preferring to use public transport whenever possible. Right now she was holding Pearl, Cal's favourite surfboard, between her knees. She had tried to insist that Cal left the board behind.

"But it's my Pearl," he'd said, shocked. "She's like another limb! I've barrelled a tube for, like, nine seconds on this board. And I was hanging ten out there at Newquay on Pearl when I met Doris! Pearl's my lucky charm!"

"Team MacNamara. Are we all present and correct?" Aunty Mad beamed at Miranda and Cal, buried under their bags.

"Sort of," mumbled Miranda, who was hiding under her hair.

"And Cal." Aunty Mad's voice softened as she gazed at her favourite great-nephew. "Are you geared up and ready, my darling?"

"Yeah," said Cal listlessly as he gazed out of the window. "Missing my babe," he whispered.

"It's been less than a day since you saw Doris," snapped Miranda.

"Jackie, are you looking forward to your new school?" Aunty went on.

"I'm not talking," he replied from the footwell, where he

was lurking with Fester.

"You'll be nice to Fester, won't you, Aunty?" Miranda said anxiously.

Aunty hesitated. "I never went for the Man's Best Friend thing. But I expect we'll learn to tolerate each other."

Miranda pressed her cheek against the glass and watched an aeroplane trawl across the sky. She'd found it hard to speak to her parents yesterday. She couldn't shake the feeling they were abandoning them. She'd been cool and quiet even when Pinkie-Sue had burst into tears and had run back from the car to give them all a last hug.

"I love you all very much, and we'll be back before you know it," she said. "Lots of children go to boarding school."

Miranda had allowed herself to be embraced, and then she'd taken Jackie's hand and pulled him back from his mother.

"Goodbye," she said stiffly, and led him away.

The children had been allowed to pack two trunks each, one full of clothes and one smaller trunk of *things*.

Miranda had taken her phone, some books and her laptop. She'd also taken her recent copies of *Autotrader*, her photo albums – mostly pictures of seals – and her fins, just in case she had a chance to use them.

Jackie had a Thermos flask of seawater and a plastic bag full of sand.

"I can recreate the beach," he said. He also had a mobile phone which Cal had given him and the bank details of all his parents' accounts.

Cal had two wetsuits, his surfboard, and a photograph of Doris in a bikini.

Aunty Mad chattered on as the bus chugged through the streets.

"Such a cold place, that hotel," she was saying. "Pinkie had to keep the fires burning all the time. And the guests were SO demanding."

Miranda was not in the mood for this. She fingered her mobile phone and wondered if you were allowed to text people on aeroplanes.

"And you, Cal," said Aunty. "In the sea every minute of the day. Your parents were constantly fretting about you out there. I'm glad that you're going to spend more time on dry land. You need to develop some new interests besides surfing and girls."

"Maybe I do," Cal agreed. "But those things are pretty hard to beat."

"Miranda, that mermaid job! *Such* a peculiar idea. Glittery tails and bikini tops don't promote you as a serious individual. Nor does your prepubescent obsession with motors."

Miranda, sucking her salty hair, emitted a low growl.

"She's not prepubescent, she's got a bra. It's a 32 double A," announced Jackie loudly.

"SHUT UP, BIG MOUTH." Miranda punched Jackie's back.

Aunty Mad didn't appear to notice.

"And Jackie, a stint at a decent school is just what you need. You can't hide behind this feral child thing any more. You need to learn to relate to people. . ." She caught sight of the children's stony faces. "I only say these things because I want you all to grow up to be the best human beings you possibly can and your old school was SO crowded and. . ."

"I will miss the earwigs," announced Jackie in a shaky voice. "And it's always funny when the guests stand on a slug."

Miranda spat out her hair. "What about the time a bat fell out of the ceiling of the restaurant, and everyone thought it was a manifestation of Hugo?"

The children were off, reminiscing about the hotel and the good times.

"St Anne's will sort you out," said Aunty Mad. "The head is possibly over-strict but a wall of discipline, underscoring of traditional values and firm boundaries are just what you three need."

Miranda pulled a face. "A wall of discipline?"

Cal shrugged. "I thought you were into the free groove, Aunty M."

Aunty Mad grimaced, giving herself three extra chins.

"Free grooving didn't get me anywhere," she stated. "Nor will it you."

"There is no wall that cannot be breached," said Jackie.

CHAPTER SIX

The Parting of
Fester and Jackie

When the children arrived at the station, Miranda noticed a sleepy-looking girl of about fifteen dragging a suitcase and wearing a maroon skirt and checked blouse. Miranda recognized the clothes. It was the St Anne's school uniform; their new school uniform.

"Check out the representative from The Wall of Discipline," said Cal. "That chick may know her boundaries but she can't do up her shoelaces."

"We're supposed to be in drag," said Jackie, also spotting her. Miranda could have kicked herself. Of course they should be wearing uniforms. Why hadn't any of them thought of it? There was a bag somewhere which had the uniforms inside, still in their wrappers.

The family had to get off the train at Barnstaple, where

a teacher was supposed to meet them. Then, another bus journey before they reached the school. Aunty wasn't coming; she had a meeting later that morning about building a community compost toilet, and as Cal was nearly seventeen and therefore Responsible, the children were travelling on the train by themselves.

Miranda spied two more girls in St Anne's school uniform. They were aged about sixteen, with shiny hair and sparkling shoes. Miranda hid behind Cal as they entered the ticket hall. The girl caught sight of Cal sauntering past and looked at his black hair tied back with string and admired his long brown legs in his green surf shorts. She nudged her friend and their eyes widened. Miranda smiled in pride at the effect her brother was having on these girls.

She hurried after her family and noticed to her dismay that Fester was still trotting along behind Jackie. This was bad. They should have tied him up outside. Yesterday, before Mum left, she'd said that under no circumstances should Fester come to the train station with them, because it would be too much for Jackie. But this morning, no one had wanted to take him out of Jackie's arms.

At the top of the steps, a station worker in a peaked cap stepped out in front of them.

"No dogs on the platform, unless he's travelling," he said.

Jackie looked stricken.

"Couldn't you bend the rules, just this once?" begged Aunty Mad.

"No," said the railway man. He didn't leave them, but

watched to see what they would do. He had thick legs and his eyelids were large and baggy.

"I'll take Fester back now," said Aunty, clutching his collar. Jackie fell to his knees, hugging his dog. Miranda touched her brother's back. She felt pretty shaky herself.

"Don't," said Jackie in a broken little voice. "Don't take my dog away."

"She's only a dog," said Aunty, desperately looking round for help.

"It's a HE," sobbed Jackie.

"Just go," Miranda told her aunt.

But Jackie let out a howl. "No. Don't do this to me."

"Stop it, Jackie," said Aunty. "You'll see it, I mean her, I mean him, in a few weeks when I come to visit." She patted the dog on his head, then wiped her hands on her skirt. Jackie grasped Fester even tighter. His shoulders started heaving, like he was going to be sick. Miranda leaned down to cuddle her brother and she felt his small solid body trembling. Cal ruffled Jackie's hair.

"Time to go, bro," he said, helping him to his feet. "Now kiss Aunty."

Jackie shook his head.

"Wipe your nose." Cal gave his little brother a tissue and as Jackie mopped his face, Cal grabbed his surfboard and unclipped the leash, which he then fixed to Fester's collar.

Cal held Jackie's shoulders. "He'll be fine. Just think! No cleaning up turds. No flea bites or worm breath in your face in the mornings." Cal handed Aunty the leash and marched Jackie down the platform.

"Cal is such a good lad," said Aunty in a trembling voice. "I wish I could have you all live in my flat, but you would drive me insane. . ."

"We'll be OK," said Miranda, giving her a hug. She hefted everyone's luggage plus Cal's surfboard on to the trolley and sped off the platform after her brothers. Then she hurried back to kiss Fester.

"Ring you tonight," she called, and ran off again.

For a moment Miranda stopped and looked around her. She watched the passengers rushing past. She couldn't see anyone she knew. Aunty and Fester had gone, Cal and Jackie were out of sight and her parents were thousands of miles away. Miranda pulled out her emergency mobile phone and dialled her mother's number. The answerphone kicked in.

This is Pinkie-Sue MacNamara's answering machine. Though I am not a machine, sometimes I feel like one. . .

Miranda listened to it all because she wanted to hear her mother's voice.

When it was finished she set off to find her brothers. She walked past the girls she had seen earlier. The girls all looked immaculate: perfect hair, fashionable shoes, expensive bags. Miranda looked down at her grubby jeans and Cal's old faded orange sweatshirt. She probably hadn't brushed her hair for at least three days. The train swished in behind her, making her jump, and slid to a halt, smelling of diesel and overheated people. The doors fell open and passengers spilled out, clogging up the platform.

Where were the boys?

Oh good, there was Jackie, haring up and down the platform, right on the white line you're not supposed to cross in case you get sucked into the slipstream and pulverized into a million bloody pieces on the track. But where had he got the red coat? Miranda realized the boy she was watching wasn't Jackie at all. Her brothers ought to be at the far end of the train. They had reserved seats and their train was due to leave in five minutes. But Miranda didn't want to get on without the boys.

"Hey, Miranda!" Cal materialized just ahead of her, but her relief was short-lived.

"Is little bro with you?"

"No," replied Miranda. "He's with you."

"Uh uh." Cal rubbed his chin. "We were in the sugar queue and then he, like, wasn't. Slippery dude."

"Oh hell." Miranda looked round the station. "Have you checked the loos?"

Cal nodded.

"The waiting room?"

"Uh huh."

Miranda groaned as a thought struck her. "You don't think he's gone after Fester?"

"Good call," said Cal. "If so, Mad will bring him back pronto."

There was an announcement that the train would be leaving shortly, so they decided to split up and search the cafe, the ladies' room, and the length of the platform.

"I'll meet you in two, back here, on this exact spot," said

Cal. "Do not get on the train without me." Miranda ran down the platform, her heart pounding. How could this have happened? Jackie never ran away. She corrected herself. Actually he did, but never at an important time like this. Only when he had to go to the dentist, or when Granny MacNamara was coming over, or on the first day at school, and the second, and the third, and when the environmental health inspector was coming round, and at Christmas last year when he had forgotten to get anyone any presents.

Miranda was feeling more and more panicky. They couldn't miss this train. The teacher would be expecting them at the other end.

She watched the St Anne's girls climb aboard.

"Are you getting on?" the baggy-eyed guard asked her, looking at all the luggage. "Hurry up."

To her relief, Miranda caught sight of Cal's dark handsome head, bobbing through the crowd. He reached her just as the guard was busy slamming doors all up the train.

But Cal was alone.

CHAPTER SEVEN

Jackie and Fester Reunite

"Check the train," yelled Miranda, running down the platform, peering into the carriages and ignoring the funny looks from the people sitting inside.

"He wouldn't get on without us," panted Cal, dragging the trolley after him.

"I've got the tickets, all his stuff. He doesn't even know which train we're riding."

The last door slammed and the guard blew his whistle. He shouted at them to step back. Then he blew his whistle again and the train pulled away.

"Ahhh," said Cal. "We bailed on that one."

"Speak normally," snapped Miranda. "We're not on the beach now."

"Don't gnarl up on me, babe," her brother replied.

"We have to think," Miranda said, but panic was clouding her brains.

"Jackie," shouted Cal. "Where are you hiding, buddy?"

"Why did you let him out of your sight?" Miranda growled.

"It's not my fault," said Cal, looking hurt. "You know what a freaky kid he is."

Now the train was just a twisting line in the distance.

"You think he's gone home?" asked Cal.

"We haven't got a home," replied Miranda stiffly.

"Let's check out the car park," said Cal.

They hurried back over the platform, abandoned the trolley and bumped their bags down the steps.

"When do we tell someone?" asked Miranda. "Should I phone Aunty?"

Cal shook his head and heaved his surfboard under his arm. "We don't know if he's properly lost yet. And what use would Aunty be? She'll come walling back here and mess things up even more. Let's search the place first."

Miranda glanced around the newsagent's shop.

"Look," she screeched. On the seating area just inside the entrance of the station was Fester's tartan collar and Cal's surfboard leash.

Miranda picked it up. What did this mean? Was the dog missing as well as her brother?

Just then Miranda's mobile phone rang.

Aunty!

"Are you on the train?" Aunty Mad asked, sounding

47

flustered and out of breath.

Miranda thought quickly. "Nearly," she said. After all, as soon as they found Jackie, they'd catch the next one.

"But it should have left three minutes ago," said Aunty.

"Delayed," said Miranda. She hesitated, stroking the collar with her thumb. "Is Fester with you?"

Aunty paused. "Ye-es," she said slowly.

Liar.

"Got to go, Aunty," said Miranda. "Must go get ourselves some traditional boundaries." She was beginning to get an idea of what might have happened.

Miranda's phone rang again.

"Miranda, it's me." The gruff voice could only belong to her little brother. In the background she heard a squeaky whine.

"Listen," said Jackie. "I'm not going to that school and Fester says he doesn't want to stay at Aunty's. Don't worry about us. We'll be fine."

As she listened, Cal grabbed Miranda and dragged her behind an advertisement hoarding. He gestured at her to look round and she saw Aunty up above them in the station car park, poking around in some nettles.

"Fester?" she was calling. "Where are you, you hideous hound?"

Miranda spoke back into the phone. "I'm going to tell Aunty."

"Do what you like," said Jackie. "I'm going home. See for yourself. Look in the top of the bus over the road." As the phone went dead, a double-decker bus drew past. A small tousle-headed figure waved at her from the top window. Fester, sitting on Jackie's lap, slobbered over the glass. Both of them looked very pleased with themselves.

"Stop!" cried Miranda. But of course it didn't. The bus was the number nine. It would take Jackie back to St Austell. From there he could catch another bus to the sea.

"He says he's going home," she said and felt her legs go weak. Cal leaned on his board.

"Home?"

Miranda shrugged.

"Maybe he's gone home, home," said Cal.

"But there's nobody there," said Miranda. "Unless you count Victorian Hugo, which I don't. Because he isn't."

"For sure," said Cal. "That's just how Jackie would like it."

As they watched from their hiding place, Aunty Mad swore and scurried down the steps to the taxi rank.

"Do we tell her. . .?" Miranda held her breath as Mad climbed in a taxi and was driven off.

"I guess not," said Cal. He folded his arms and smiled at her. "We have a situation," he said.

One of the things Miranda loved about her brother was that he never panicked. Even at times such as now, when panicking was logical.

"Dad is going to be axed . . . greatly displeased about this," said Cal.

Cormac hadn't yet forgiven Jackie for the cliff-climbing

escapade. Cormac said he had aged ten years that night. This new stunt would finish him off.

Cal bent to pick up the luggage.

"Come on," he said. "We're going home too."

CHAPTER EiGHT

The Dodo Lives Again

Cal and Miranda stood on the windy cliff clutching their luggage. The weather had turned and the wind buffed them. The sea pounded the rocks. Miranda hoped Mica was safe.

And there was The Dodo Hotel, the sand whipping up the walls of The Circus. Was it really only twenty-four hours since they had left? The tide was right in, slapping up against the pebbles.

Miranda felt her stomach tighten. Please let Jackie be inside. Cal, however, was looking longingly at the breakers as he hid the suitcases behind a gorse bush.

"Focus," said Miranda, hauling at her brother's arm. They crossed the empty hotel car park, stepped over the smooth mud path and started the rocky descent to the beach.

Cal was half talking to himself.

"When we've got brah, we'll get the bus and another train and then taxi right into The Wall of Discipline and no one will ever know about this slip."

Miranda thought it all sounded doable. Aunty, Cormac and Pinkie-Sue would never need to know.

They slipped through the metal fence where it met the cliff, and trod softly through the garden. They slipped round the back of the building, passing the washing line, the abandoned barbecue and the periwinkled grave of Brickie, their first dog. It was all still here, like it had been waiting for them to come back. Miranda shivered. It was exactly the same, and yet completely different. The huge rugosa rose by the back door had shed all its flowers. This was strange. Yesterday, when the family had left (was it really only yesterday?) the bush had been in full bloom. Now pink petals blew over the garden. The back door of the hotel hadn't been boarded up because it was made from the steel door of an old warship.

Miranda froze. A large, unfamiliar pair of men's trainers stood on the doorstep. A cold trickle of fear ran down her back.

Cal eyed the shoes and looked at Miranda.

"Intruder?"

"What about Jackie?" she whispered.

"Come on." Cal stepped over the trainers.

"How do we get in?" asked Miranda.

Cal looked puzzled. "I've still got my keys. Haven't you

got yours?"

Of course she still had them. No one had suggested she give them to anyone.

She yelped as something large crashed out from the rugosa and rolled to her feet.

"Thanks for the adrenalin fix, bro," said Cal.

It was Jackie, puffing and blowing, with Fester simpering at his feet.

"Don't go in." Jackie's mouth was smeared with chocolate and his hair was stuck with rose petals. Miranda fell to her knees and hugged him. She shut her eyes in relief.

"Nutcase," she said. "What a day to wig out. . ."

"There's someone in there," interrupted Jackie. "I saw his shadow through the window."

The children conferred behind the rugosa. If they contacted the police it would lead to awkward questions about what they were doing here. But none of them wanted to walk away and leave the intruder snooping round.

Cal stood up decisively. "I'm going to see who this guy is."

"No," said Jackie, grabbing his arm. "He might be a violent psychopath with a deep-seated hatred of surfers."

"You're stronger on imagination than you are on school attendance, dude," replied Cal. He fitted his key into the lock and pushed open the heavy door.

"Things keep happening," grumbled Jackie.

"It's your fault," retorted Miranda.

"Bring on some hush," said Cal. He frowned at them.

53

"Guys, stay outside."

"No way," said Jackie. Miranda felt scared but she wasn't going to be left out.

It was gloomy inside the back hallway until Jackie thoughtlessly switched on the light. The children crept up the corridor, stepping over marks in the carpet where furniture had been removed. There was a clattering coming from the hotel kitchen. Miranda bit her lip. They shouldn't be here. She felt scared but also annoyed. Who dared to trespass in their home?

"Whoa," whispered Cal. He gestured to the back door. "Out," he mouthed.

Miranda vigorously shook her head. They tiptoed towards the noise, Jackie dragging on her sleeve.

"Do you have a plan?" Miranda asked her older brother softly.

"I'll go in first. If he looks like a violent psychopath, beat it," whispered Cal.

The hotel kitchen was situated at the back of the hotel. It was a big, wide room with two sets of doors: one set led out to the restaurant and the other to the corridor in which the children were now standing.

"Keep together," said Miranda quietly.

They stepped into the room just as the far door swung shut.

The Violent Psychopath had just left.

The kitchen tap dripped and the counter was still damp where the Violent Psychopath had just wiped it. A pile of dust sat in the centre of the floor where the Violent

54

Psychopath had swept up.

"This sure is one house-proud burglar," whispered Cal. "Oh!" He picked something off the floor.

"What is it?" Miranda looked at a tiny gold swallow in Cal's palm.

Her brother's face broke out into a delighted smile and he raced from the kitchen into the dining area.

"Dude? Is that you?"

"Who's Dude?" asked Jackie.

Miranda shrugged. "Could be anyone."

There was a crash and the pair looked at each other. Fester whined.

"TOTALLY AMPED," screamed Cal.

"Is he being murdered?" asked Jackie, looking scared.

"I'm not sure." Miranda cautiously put her face to the window in the door.

The dining room was dark because the windows had been boarded up, but she could see Cal with someone. He was either fighting or hugging them, surrounded by the dust-sheeted tables and chairs.

The person was smaller than he. And when Cal turned Miranda saw a mass of golden curls.

"It's Doris!" shouted Miranda. She pushed through the door with Jackie thundering after her. Doris was wearing a green cardigan, a yellow skirt and no shoes. Her eyes were red and her face all puffy, like she'd been crying.

Everyone looked at one another.

"You're not supposed to be here," said Doris in a squeaky

55

voice.

"Nor are you," said Miranda. She rushed forward, knocking an upturned chair off a table, and hugged her.

"This is seriously embarrassing," said Doris.

Cal took her hand, a huge, soppy smile on his face. "Awesome," he said, and leaned in to kiss her. Miranda and Jackie rolled their eyes at each other and Fester whined.

Cal waved his hand behind him, mid-snog. "Cool it, canine, this is epic."

A few minutes later, now with everyone sitting on the carpet, Doris explained.

"It's pretty twisted of me," she began.

"We like twisty," said Jackie.

"I was at home and I was sad, missing you guys." She gazed mistily at Cal. "Mum said something that upset me, and I had to get out. Like Now. I just put whatever shoes I could find on my feet and got on my bike and rode up here."

That would explain the men's trainers on the doorstep, thought Miranda. Doris was renowned for various odd behaviours, like the time she knitted Fester a jumper, or glued thousands of little shells to her mother's car door.

"Where's your bike now?" asked Jackie.

"In the hedge," replied Doris. "I'm so sorry, you guys. I didn't mean to break in. I had a key and I just wanted to be here, y'know?"

They all did.

"Action babe," said Cal softly.

"I missed you so much." Doris swallowed and put a

tissue to her eyes. "I couldn't bear it without you."

Jackie and Miranda exchanged a grimace.

"I've been, like, lost," whispered Doris.

"Me too," said Cal softly. "I'm so on your level."

"It's been less than twenty-four hours," said Miranda tartly.

"But what about you guys?" asked Doris, dragging her gaze from Cal's handsome face. She looked at her watch. "It's five-fifteen p.m. You should have arrived at your school an hour ago. According to the school website you would be eating your evening meal. Tonight's menu was supposed to be buttered potatoes, pork and asparagus and peas."

"You looked all that up?" laughed Cal.

Doris looked sheepish. "I did it to feel close to you. I've been time-tabling everything."

"Sweet," said Cal, and squeezed her hand.

"Stalker," muttered Jackie.

"You still haven't told me why you're here," said Doris.

Miranda found a cushion from under a dust sheet and got comfortable. "Where do we begin?"

"So – you're runaways," said Doris, five minutes later.

"No way," said Jackie. "How can we be runaways when we've only run home?" He moved round the room, removing the dust sheets from the furniture. His hair was sticking together, as something viscous had reached his fringe and congealed there.

"But why?" Doris was asking Jackie.

"Fester," replied Jackie. "Aunty was taking him away. I

couldn't stand it." Fester squirmed under a table, wagging his tail guiltily and looking out at everyone from under his furry eyebrows and unable to believe his luck. He was normally banished from the dining room. Jackie stroked the dog's head. "They can't take my dog away," he said. "I'm staying here."

"Jackie, you meathead," said Cal. "You know The Dodo is for sale."

Jackie smiled. "I sorted that already." He pretended to pick up a phone. He dialled a number and put a finger to his lips and waited. He cleared his throat and lowered his voice to a growl.

"*Is that Messieurs Oliver and co? This is Cormac MacNamara at The Dodo Hotel. I'm ringing to inform you that we are taking the hotel off the market. Thank you so much for your help and we are sorry for any inconvenience.*"

Jackie put the pretend phone down.

"You didn't do that," said Miranda, marvelling at her brother's capacity for anarchy.

"I did it on the bus," said Jackie. "I knew I had to crack on as there's no mobile signal here." He smiled contentedly.

"I bet you're pleased," Jackie grinned. He had the sort of smile that made you want to join in. "It should stop any buyers coming round."

"Bruddah, maybe you need those boundaries after all," sighed Cal.

Miranda looked at her little brother, innocently ruffling Fester's ears. "Jackie, what about school? The Wall of Discipline? Mum and Dad? Money? What about People?"

"Don't sweat the small stuff," said Jackie. He turned to Cal. "If we do this right, we could stay here for another couple of weeks at least. That should give the elders time to sort out their messes. We may never have to go to that bloodsucking school."

"Why bloodsucking?" asked Cal, trying to look serious.

"They wanted a blood sample upon arrival," said Jackie. "Didn't you read the small print?"

"Nobody reads small print. That's why it's small," chipped in Doris. "It's not small to save trees, you know."

Everyone looked at her.

"And that's me over and out," she said.

Cal stretched out his legs. "Jackie, we've got to contact the school and let them know we're going to be late. They'll be wondering why we didn't get off that train. They may have already phoned Aunty." He looked uncharacteristically serious.

"I've already contacted them," replied Jackie. He frowned and pursed his lips.

"*Hello, is that St Anne's? Can I speak to Mrs Pearson? This is Pinkie-Sue MacNamara, mother of Callum, Miranda and Jack MacNamara. Yes, that's right, the late applications, well I'm so sorry, but we have had to change our plans, yes, yes, no they're not coming, no. We are staying in the country . . . at the same address, yes, it was too much for the children. Of course you can keep the deposit, yes, yes, yes. . .*" Jackie's voice trailed off.

"You didn't," breathed Miranda in awe. How did he think of these things?

"I did," said Jackie smugly. "Some people are so gullible."

"But you're telling lies," said Miranda.

"Estate agents always tell lies," said Jackie. "I heard Mum say so."

"But. . ."

"It's done," said Jackie. "It was easy. I don't know why all children don't do it."

"Because it's mad," said Miranda, trying to conceal her admiration.

Jackie frowned. "Don't tell me you're not the teeniest bit pleased that we're here?"

Miranda was delighted to be here. She was home! Home! HOME!

"What's the worst that can happen?" Jackie sniffed. "We get into big trouble and get deported back to St Alcatraz. I'm always getting into trouble. This is slightly bigger trouble than usual, but it's worth it. We're not doing anyone any harm. No one is worried about us."

"What if Mum and Dad phone the school?" asked Miranda.

"They won't for ages." Cal spoke up. "They'll phone Aunty. At the moment they're still in the air, or just landed. We need to email them and say that school doesn't allow mobile phones," he went on. "Tell them only to email us. In fact, why don't we email them now? I'm pretty sure it's still connected up."

"My laptop is in my bag," said Miranda. "But I'm not going to email lies. . ."

"Just out of interest, what was supposed to be for pudding at St Anne's?" Jackie asked Doris. He had lost interest in the present conversation.

"Blackberry and apple pie with a choice of custard, cream, or double cream," said Doris.

Jackie's stomach let out an enormous rumble. "Have we got any food?" he asked.

"Only the End of the World Food," said Miranda.

The End of the World Food was a box of tins that Pinkie-Sue kept under the back stairs. In this box were cans and cans of baked beans, Spam, fruit cocktail and peas. It was all at least five years old.

"Guys, that stuff is stale. We could be like foragers? We could gather some mussels and seaweed from the beach and make a stew," said Cal.

"Or you could cycle up to Burger World," suggested Jackie.

There was a fast food cafe next to the garage on the St Austell road roundabout four miles away.

"That's a better plan," agreed Cal. He looked at Doris. "Coming with me, dude?"

"Cal. . ." began Miranda.

"Our beds are still here, right?" mused Cal.

Miranda nodded.

"So we may as well stay just for one night. No one will be missing us yet." He paused. "Listen to the wind. We could even catch a wave or two."

Miranda stared at her brother with growing excitement. Was this possible?

"I'll go get the food," said Cal. He touched Miranda's nose. "You look slightly crazy, sister. Why don't you send the email, then go outside and check on your furry buddies?"

Miranda's laptop lay open in front of her on the steel work surface, which was grubbier than it had ever been before. It was piled with food wrappings and plastic forks. Cal had cycled off to the cafe with Doris and come back laden with food. The staff at Burger Palace seemed to change every few weeks and no one had recognized Cal. The burgers and fries had been absolutely delicious but now Miranda felt full of grease.

> Hey, folks! All well. We arrived safely. It is nice here. Email is the best way to communicate. Don't try to phone, there are phone politics. We will call you.
> The boys are happy, though everything is quite weird.
> Kisses
> M, C and J.
> XXX

Miranda clicked on SEND. None of it was An Actual Lie. She was turning into a con artist like Jackie. She shut her laptop. What now? As she wandered round the ground floor she felt a rush of energy. She liked listening to the pipes gurgle after she'd switched the boiler back on. It was all so comfortable, and so familiar, but very soon the world would catch up with them and they would be shipped off to school. She listened to the waves outside. They would have to take the boards off a couple of the lower windows in the dining room so they could see out. In the kitchen she eyed the food leftovers piled into the sink and decided that runaways did not clear up. Instead she ran out into the garden and round to the beach.

Miranda stood in a foot of clear, salty water, watching the seaweed swirl round her ankles. Far out to sea, Cal and Doris were riding the waves. Jackie and Fester were digging on the other side of the beach, just under the waterfall path, which was the other way to get down to Dummity Bay.

A figure was walking northwards along the cliff edge. It was a tallish man with short black hair and a big rucksack. He had a pair of binoculars round his neck. Miranda didn't recognize him. He was probably just a hiker. But they'd have to be careful. Ned Kile walked his dog every morning on the beach at seven o'clock and he knew they were supposed to be away at school. And there would be others. She decided not to worry.

"Mica, Hugo, Pasty, Alice, Grandma, I'm back," she called.

This was a dream come true.

CHAPTER NINE

The Gift from the Sea

Something wasn't right. Miranda opened her eyes. She was lying under a yellow guest duvet. Where was her ancient flowery eiderdown? Then she remembered it was in storage. Miranda sat up as the events of the previous day crowded into her head, and she pulled the duvet up over her face in order to block them out. It didn't work. The scale of what they had done yesterday was bigger than any bad deed they had done before. Miranda did not know what the day would bring, but she was sure that by the end of it, Fester would be stationed with Aunty and they would be incarcerated in St Anne's. They'd become the first children to get into deep trouble with the school before they'd even arrived. They might even get expelled. (Was this technically possible?)

Despite all this, Miranda couldn't help a huge grin stretching over her face. She was home! She got out of bed, crossed the floor and parted the curtains (*her* curtains; turquoise flowers on a light blue background). Sun rays poured into the sea as a light wind rolled the waves. The beach was deserted apart from the herring gulls gliding round the cliffs. Yesterday evening she'd seen all five seals resting on the rocks. Mica had seemed a bit thin compared to the others, but able to waddle quickly out of the way when Hugo had started barking and throwing his weight around.

Miranda paused on the stairs. Usually at this time of day the hotel was awash with sounds: the breakfast waitress arriving, the water pumping as guests took their early morning showers, the phone ringing, the creaks and whines of the cliff winch as food or laundry was delivered, but now all Miranda could hear was the wind worrying the window frames and the rush of the sea. Five minutes later and she was lying flat on Cal's spare board, paddling out to the deep water and thinking how nice it was not having anyone nagging her to do her teeth or eat breakfast before anything interesting could happen. Her wetsuit had been in the outhouse as usual. She had forgotten to pack it, which was a good thing because the water was chilly. The waves were beating her back to shore and it felt like she wasn't getting anywhere. Miranda gave up and lay back on her surf board, rolling with the swell, when Cal popped up beside her, water streaming off his head.

"I didn't see you!" she gasped as he grabbed her board.

He was wearing a mask and snorkel, which he pushed up

on to his forehead as he trod water beside her. "I've found something," he panted. "Come over here." He towed her towards the cliffs. When he'd swum a little way, he stopped and repositioned his mask. "Wait," he said, and dived. His flippers beat the surface and he was gone. Miranda peered down – the bottom was ten feet away, maybe less. She watched Cal's blurry red outline, and then she saw a large dark mass. It was about the size of a car, but it was hard to tell as the water magnified everything. A wave caught her and tipped her right over into the sea. Miranda clenched her teeth as the cold water got into her ears.

When she rose, Cal was waiting for her.

"Take this," he said, handing her his mask. Miranda positioned it over her eyes. Then she unhooked her leash from her ankle and passed it to Cal.

Cal pointed down. "See what you think."

Miranda took a lungful of air and dived. The greeny water swirled past her, thick with little stones that had been churned up by the current, and she felt herself dragged inland as her hands landed on something hard and flat. It was some kind of container. Another fierce pull and the whole box moved, banging into Miranda's arm. She felt a tug on her other arm and looked up to see Cal dragging her to the surface.

"It's too rough," he coughed as they broke the surface.

Miranda grabbed her board and hung in the water. Her arm was stinging with pain where the crate had knocked her.

"What is it?" she gasped.

"We'll find out before the end of the day," said Cal, bobbing beside her. "It's coming inshore fast." He looked out to sea at the swell. "Come on, time to go in."

Back in the hotel, Miranda found Jackie perched on the table, feeding the remains of last night's fries to Fester.

"We're running out of food," he yawned. His face was still smeared with grime. Someone ought to persuade him to wash today. How did Pinkie-Sue do it?

Miranda opened the fridge. It was empty, of course. As were all the cupboards and the freezers. All the wine and spirits from the bar had been boxed up and left in the outhouse, but these were no use. Doris had said she would drop by today after college. She might bring some food, but she was unlikely to appear until the afternoon.

"We're going to run out of money too," Jackie said. "We might starve to death. I've lost the PIN number to Mum's account." He pointed at his sister. "You need to go and work a mermaid shift. Go and grovel and get your job back."

"I don't think Mrs Reegan would have me back," said Miranda sadly. "She took away my tail."

Cal appeared, wrapped in a blanket, steaming from the shower.

"Have you guys looked for the End of the World Food?" he suggested. "I want breakfast."

Miranda ran out of the kitchen to the stairs. She found the cardboard box and opened the lid. The cans looked a bit dusty but lots of them were still in date. There was also a tin opener. Miranda was carrying an armful of tinned beans back to the kitchen when she stopped dead. Cal had taken a few boards off the windows, including the one which looked on to The Nip. And now a man, last night's hiker, was halfway down it.

Miranda dumped the beans and hurried to the little downstairs loo at the near end of the building. She peeped through the net curtain of the tiny window to get a closer look (this window was too small to bother boarding up as no one would be able to get through). The man had gone. Miranda waited for ages, but nothing moved. She went to the main reception and looked out of the front window where Cal had removed another board. There was no one on the beach. The hiker must have gone back up The Nip. Back in the kitchen, she learned that Jackie and Fester had gone back to bed (oh the bliss of being free to do that) and Cal was sipping coffee, still wearing only a blanket and reading a surfing magazine.

"I saw a man on The Nip," she said. "I didn't recognize him. But he's gone."

"Gone is good," said Cal. "Did you find any food?"

They both jumped as the wind suddenly squalled over the roof.

"High tide is in two hours," said Cal, checking his phone. "I bet that crate will have come in by then."

"Do you think it's linked to *The Big Jesse*?" asked Miranda.

Nearly two months previously, a container ship, *The Big Jesse*, had spilled its cargo overboard, just off Devon Head. A few miles upland, crates and broken containers had ended up on Penwinger Beach. The children had biked over to watch. People had arrived and broken open metal containers and loaded stuff into vans and small trucks. They'd thrown brand-new clothes or toys all over the beach. Miranda had been frightened by how aggressive everyone had been. Like they thought it was their right to help themselves. A gang of nasty-looking lads arrived complete with metal cutting machinery and chainsaws for getting through the crates.

"Can we join in?" Jackie had looked longingly at a large tantalizing box abandoned on a dune.

"This isn't salvage, dude, it's stealing," said Cal, and he'd made Miranda and Jackie cycle home.

They learned that the police turned up eventually and mounted a guard. (There was a rumour that a policeman had been seen putting a brand-new lawnmower into the back of his police van.) The newspaper people and the TV people arrived, and for a week the whole of the bay felt under siege. Eventually the shipping company came to claim the remains and everyone went away and nothing was left but a few ashy places where the scavengers had lit bonfires.

Miranda didn't want all that coming to their little beach. Especially not now.

After a whole can of beans each, Miranda and Cal waded back into the sea. Cal had a rope slung over his shoulder. They scanned the water, looking for any clues; then Miranda saw a dark line washing just beyond the surf. She pointed it out to Cal and they splashed over. A wooden crate, black with sea slime, was being tugged by the waves to the shore. It was bound with metal bands and the gaps between the panels were coated with rubbery stuff. It was about three metres long and half as wide.

Miranda touched the wood and it was firm. Stuff which floated in with the tide usually just crumbled under your fingers if it had been in the sea for too long. She examined the metal ties.

"We'll need bolt croppers for those," said Cal. He wound the rope round the crate and gave one end to his sister.

"Heave ho," he said, and together they hauled in the crate with the tide. It slid surprisingly easily over the smooth sand. And they managed to drag it behind the Whale Stone before it got stuck in deep wet sand and would not budge.

"This is hopeless," puffed Miranda. Her arms ached from all the pulling.

Cal gave her a look. "Shall we open it, just to see?"

"I'll see if the bolt croppers are still in the shed," said Miranda.

Five minutes later she was back, dragging the heavy tool bag behind her in the sand. Her parents had left so much stuff behind. Maybe they were secretly planning to come back.

"Hurry up, chick!" yelled Cal, who was sitting on the box. He jumped down into the shallow water and ran over to his sister. He took the bag from her and heaved it up on to the crate.

"Bolt cropper, screwdriver, saw, axe and a hammer," said Miranda.

Cal took the croppers and fastened them over the metal band. With a clunk, he snipped it open and the metal sprang apart, slicing into the water and narrowly missing Miranda's face.

"Stand back," said Cal, already positioning himself for the next bracket. The water lapped around Miranda's legs as she watched her brother work. What could be inside? More importantly, who did it belong to? She told herself that they were not stealing the box, merely looking inside. They were not like the scavengers of Penwinger Beach. After Cal had broken open the last band, Miranda joined Cal on top of the box. By now, three herring gulls had discovered them, and were also interested in the contents.

"We should wait until the tide goes out before we open it," said Miranda, shooing away an especially persistent gull as it perched on the crate. "The water might damage whatever is inside."

Cal looked disappointed. "Or we could bore a teeny little hole in the top? Just to see if it's worth opening?"

"Let's do it," said Miranda, tingling with excitement.

She passed her brother the saw.

"If it has come off *The Big Jesse*, why hasn't it rotted?" asked Miranda, watching Cal cut into the wood.

"Maybe it came out of a metal container that has only just busted open," said Cal. "Or fell off some other ship."

Miranda scanned the horizon. There was nothing but a sailing boat, way out to sea. Cal, now sweating, had sawed a small hole in the box and was working from the other direction. The saw was blunt and the teeth kept catching in the wet wood. Miranda anxiously checked the beach for people. Cal grunted as a length of wood fell away. He knelt and peered inside the crate. "AWESOME!" He sat up, his mouth open. Miranda pushed past him and leaned into the hole. It was hard to see what it was, because the contents were densely wrapped in plastic, and there was padding material stuffed into all the gaps. She waited impatiently as Cal cut away some of the plastic with the saw. Then she glimpsed a shine of black metal, and then large handlebars. As Cal pulled away a big length of plastic she saw a padded, red area – a seat!

"What is it?" asked Miranda, jiggling up and down. "A quad bike?"

"It's better than that," said Cal. "It's a PWC."

Miranda looked again. "A what?"

"Personal water craft. A jet ski," said Cal. "Oooh ooh ooh." He put his head right into the box.

"But it's huge." Miranda had been on a jet ski on her twelfth birthday but it had been much smaller than this one.

"It's got room for two people," came Cal's muffled voice. There was the sound of more plastic ripping. "It's a Kawasaki Tandem. A 260, with supercharger. Hello, honey!" Cal reappeared and gave Miranda a look.

"We couldn't ride it," she said. "Could we?"

"No," said Cal firmly. "That would be crazy."

They decided not to leave the jet ski on the beach. It might get damaged, or stolen.

"So now we ought to inform the police," said Cal reluctantly.

"Unless this is from *The Big Jesse*," said Miranda. "In which case no one would be looking for it."

Goods from *The Big Jesse* had been taken all over the country. There had been quad bikes and designer clothes, chainsaws, machine parts, whole cars, motorbikes, toys and computer equipment. No one knew for sure what was missing because nobody seemed to know what was supposed to be in all the shipping containers.

Miranda looked at the water swirling round the crate. Small brown fish were nibbling at the wood and darting away in the currents. "It's like a gift from the sea," she said dreamily. More than anything she wanted to unpack this thing, try to get it going, and have a ride over the bay.

"Let's get it out of the water. The boat trailer is still in the outhouse. We can move it on that," said Cal. "We'll work out what to do with it later."

For the next hour, they worked with hammers and saws, pulling away the planks that surrounded the machine. It had black padded seats and red paintwork and it gleamed with newness. Miranda thought it looked like a motorbike with a sledge instead of wheels. She and Cal fetched the boat trailer and wheeled it down the beach and behind the Whale Stone, where the jet ski waited in the shallows.

"Wow, wow, wow!" said Miranda, touching the handlebars and working the throttle.

"It's not ours," warned Cal.

"It's salvage," said Miranda.

"Merchant Shipping Act 1995, *salvage remains the property of the original owner*," quoted Cal. "And we are legally obliged to report it."

"Boring," said Miranda. Her brother was usually right about these things.

"But I don't see why we need to report it straight away," said Cal, his eyes gleaming.

"Because that would be like reporting ourselves," said Miranda. "Let's see if we can get it into the outhouse."

"No chance," said Cal. "Our best bet, if we wanted to hide it (not that we are hiding it) would be to drag it into the Seal Cave." This cave opened in the cliff behind the beach rocks. At high tide the sea went right into it, burrowing deep into the cliff, but if you kept walking back, you came to an area of fine dry sand and flat rocks, where the sea never reached. It was naturally very dark back here, with only a sprinkle of light seeping in through the tunnel from the cave mouth.

It was the perfect place to hide the jet ski.

Miranda climbed on the machine and examined the controls. The speed dial went all the way up to 150K. She throttled back, and imagined bouncing over the sea. It smelled of oil and new plastic. It was astonishing that the crate hadn't leaked at all. The machine was pristine. Miranda felt her stomach churn in excitement.

"Where are the keys?" she asked casually.

"In my pocket," replied Cal, equally casually.

"Do you think it would start?" The machine was so enticing she didn't think she could stand it.

"No," her brother said. "It needs petrol."

"Shame."

"Yeah."

Cal too couldn't keep his hands off it. He was examining the engine, pulling off bits of plastic, wiping little oil spillages, buffing up the mirrors.

"It's not ours," he said, as if to convince himself.

"But we're looking after it," said Miranda firmly. "Just for a little while."

They hefted the machine out of the remains of the box and on to the ramp of the boat trailer. Using every ounce of strength they pulled it up and tipped the trailer level. The wheels rolled easily over the sand, and Cal and Miranda wound through the rocks to the entrance of the Seal Cave. Here the greenery hung down so low it almost concealed the entrance.

"I feel like a smuggler," said Cal, heaving the trailer into the cave mouth. It fitted through perfectly, with room for Miranda and Cal to stand each side.

"We need to move it above the high-tide line," said Cal, his voice echoing against the cave walls. They crept in, the cave growing darker and darker.

"This will do. Let's go and clear up the wood from the crate," said Cal.

They had left a mess on the beach. Wood lay higgledy-piggledy and scraps of plastic were blowing over the rocks, but within five minutes they'd bundled all the plastic up and had piled the wood into a heap, ready to have a bonfire later. Cal then splashed into the sea for a cool-off.

Miranda felt hungry. Would there be anything to eat in the hotel besides beans? They'd been so caught up with the jet ski she'd forgotten about the food issue. She looked

75

at The Dodo and froze. There was a large yellow suitcase sitting on the front steps of the hotel. Whose was that? Then she noticed a retro-looking motorhome in the car park on the cliff. It looked like one of those German ones with the sleeping compartment over the front seats.

Her heart started thumping.

"Jackie?" she called, breaking into a run.

She went into the hotel through the front door, noticing the lights were on and there was a jam jar of grass on the reception desk. Then she heard voices in the stairwell and put her hand to her mouth. These were adult voices.

She watched as two people came slowly down the staircase, exclaiming at the low beam and laughing at some private joke. To her amazement, Jackie was behind them. When he saw her, he put his thumbs up.

The woman was about fifty, and wore a white and red sundress and a flat sort of hat nobody wears except on television adverts. She had brown curly hair and pink lipstick. The man was of a similar age, wearing cords, a white and green striped shirt, and carrying a newspaper. He had a bulging stomach and was almost bald. When they saw Miranda they smiled, and she automatically smiled back. The couple sailed past her and went into the restaurant.

Jackie winked at her and put his finger to his lips. Miranda couldn't believe it. She knew who these people were, though she'd never met them before in her life. She'd seen the same walk, the same relaxed manner, the same odd clothes, thousands of times.

These were people on holiday. These were *guests*.

CHAPTER TEN

The Babbings Arrive

"Jackie, you total freak," Miranda whispered. "What have you done?"

Jackie gave her a serene smile. "We need cash, don't we?"

Miranda glanced at Cal, who had appeared in the doorway. "Yes, but. . ."

"Mr and Mrs Babbing, from Plymouth, booked in for two nights." With a flourish, Jackie took the day book (yet another thing that hadn't got packed) out from under the desk.

"The Babbings do not require an evening meal but would like a cooked breakfast. Oh, and Mrs Babbing doesn't want fried bread because it takes the skin off her mouth."

"We haven't got any bread," said Miranda.

"I've put them in the Yellow Room," said Jackie, ignoring

her. "I knew you'd have the cleanest sheets, so I took them off your bed."

"You've what?"

"You're quite the natural hotelier," murmured Cal.

"But we'll be found out in seconds." Miranda could feel the panic rising.

"This ought to help." Jackie placed a wad of crisp ten-pound notes on the desk. "I asked for payment in advance. There's one hundred pounds there. I said our cash machine wasn't working."

"They gave YOU one hundred pounds?"

Jackie looked offended. "I gave them a receipt. When Mr Babbing asked to speak to the manager I said he was on the toilet."

"You're mad," said Miranda.

"No, I'm rich," said Jackie. A look of concern passed over his face. "Only, can you cook the eggs in the morning because they make me feel icky."

"No," said Miranda. "You tell them right now we can't. . ."

"We can," said Jackie, "otherwise they'll think there's something fishy going on. I already had to tell them that the windows are boarded up every year because of the autumn gales. They seemed excited."

"But. . ."

"And I said the fencing was because of building work. They swallowed that too."

"Jackie. . ."

"Shhh." Cal put his finger to his lips. "They're coming back."

The door swung open and the couple entered the room.

"Any chance of a cup of tea?" asked Mrs Babbing. "The complimentary service in our room seems to be missing." She was a brown-skinned white woman with bulgy calf muscles. Miranda looked at the money on the reception desk.

"Sure," she said, rubbing sand from her arms. "Milk and sugar?"

"Yes, please," the woman smiled, patting her hair. She exchanged looks with her husband. "I hope you don't mind me asking, but who is in charge round here?"

"Me," said Cal, in a deep voice. He smiled his most charming smile at her and Miranda watched as she melted. "My dad's having a bit of a rest, so I'm afraid you'll have to rough it with us for a bit."

"Say no more," simpered Mrs Babbing. "We can look after ourselves." She giggled and winked at Jackie. Miranda frowned. Was this woman a half-wit? What else had Jackie told her?

"We're on an extended holiday," said Mr Babbing. He had a soft, watery voice and orange socks. "We've just been to Russia on a town twinning programme, but we couldn't bear to go home yet, so we're here."

"He's hoping to get some inspiration for his book," simpered Mrs Babbing. "It's ever so good."

"Oh shush," smiled Mr Babbing.

"You're writing a book?" asked Miranda politely. She was not impressed by all this book writing and wondered why so many people did it. Weren't there enough books in the world already?

"Nearly finished the first chapter," said Mr Babbing proudly.

Miranda cleared her throat. "I'll bring the tea into the restaurant."

In the kitchen Miranda saw that they had no milk (of course) and there was only one used teabag left in the sink. She boiled a saucepan of water and squeezed the teabag into it. Then she found two old powdered milk sachets under the cutlery drawer. This would do. Now they had some money, she could send Cal up to the garage on his bike for supplies.

In the restaurant, Mr and Mrs Babbing were gazing into each other's eyes and laughing quietly. When Miranda set the tea down, they didn't even notice. Miranda deftly swiped a pile of packing paper from the next table and flicked a dead earwig into the corner. Then she lit the fire. Luckily the log basket was still full of logs and the firelighters and matches, as ever, were stuffed into the alcove.

Her parents had done a really terrible job of packing.

Mrs Babbing gave a little cough. "So do you live here or just work here?"

Miranda stiffened. "A bit of both," she said.

"It's very quiet," the woman went on. "Though that's how we like it."

"It's the end of the season," said Miranda sternly.

"It's the end of September," said Mr Babbing, running his palms over his wobbly stomach. "I'd have thought a lovely place like this would have been packed. Though I admit, it's not easy to get to and I heard some funny knocking noises in the roof. Is this place haunted?"

Miranda adopted an expression she had seen on her mother when dealing with difficult guests.

"People love to make up stories," she said. "Breakfast is between eight and ten." She rose with great dignity and left the room. She found Cal sitting on the reception desk, scrutinizing Miranda's laptop.

"There's an email from Cormac and Pinkie-Sue," he said, shoving the screen towards her. It was written in capital letters. Pinkie-Sue was suspicious of digital technology and said writing emails in the upper case made her feel more in charge.

Miranda read.

DEAR EVERYONE

THE FLIGHT WAS EXCELLENT. THEY GAVE US
THE SAME LEMON BISCUITS WE SERVE WITH
MORNING COFFEE IN THE HOTEL! WE ARE NOW
IN CALIFORNIA. CAL, YOU MUST COME HERE ONE
DAY. THE WAVES ARE "AWESOME".

HOW IS SCHOOL, ARE THEY HUMAN? IS THE
FOOD EDIBLE?

AUNTY SAYS FESTER IS NO TROUBLE AT ALL.
(I KNEW HE WOULD WIN HER ROUND.) WE SPOKE
TO HER LAST NIGHT. SHE SAID SHE SAW YOU ALL
OFF. WE MISS YOU AND UNDERSTAND ABOUT
THE PHONE CALLS. PLEASE RING US SOON!

LOTS OF LOVE MUMMA AND DAD XXX

"Aunty is a lying toad," said Miranda, stroking Fester, who was pretending to be asleep under the reception desk.

"They're totally off our case," said Cal. He paused. "Do you think we could hole up here until they get back?"

Miranda leaned against the wall, regarding her brother with admiration and a tinge of alarm. How would they do it?

"I could get a temp job somewhere," mused Cal. "And I am sixteen. I'm sure I'm legally allowed to look after you guys. After all, I could join the army and get hitched if I wanted."

Miranda felt like the world was spinning around her, going faster and faster. "Are you serious?"

Cal shrugged. "This is a big wave we're on. Let's ride it for as long as we can." He gave his sister a hug. He smelled of the sea and of boy perfume.

"What have we got to lose?"

Miranda couldn't think of anything.

There was a cough from the restaurant.

"What about THEM?" Miranda pointed to the door.

"They seem weird but chilled," said Cal. "I'll get Doris to bring the breakfast stuff. We'll manage."

"But they'll want to see an adult at some point," protested Miranda.

"They've got me," said Cal. "Now if you don't mind, I'm off for a surf."

Miranda watched from her rock as the Babbings tottered up The Nip. They were going to eat in St Austell and were in high spirits. She heard snatches of song as Mr Babbing sang to his wife. She could also hear Mrs Babbing shriek with laughter. Miranda felt a tug of sadness. Cormac used to sing to their mother all the time. Miranda wondered what her parents were doing right now. She touched her swim belt, which was fastened over her wetsuit. Inside were the keys to the jet ski. She and Cal had agreed not to say anything to Jackie. It was the sort of thing he wouldn't be able to resist. Miranda didn't know if she could resist it either. It wouldn't take much to cycle up to the garage and buy a can of petrol to make the thing work.

She had left Jackie and Fester in the hotel, where her younger brother was now sweeping the sand off the front patio. He was taking his role of hotel operator very seriously and had taken to wearing a small navy blue suit and striped shirt which had been bought for him for Cormac's sister's wedding (which he'd refused to wear on the day). This outfit was in a box in the outhouse, along with a great deal of the children's clothes which they rarely wore. So whilst Miranda could only find old T-shirts and jeans, Jackie looked smarter than he had ever done in his life.

"Appearances count," he said, spitting on his hands and smoothing back his hair. He had been very diligent in the last hour, hoovering the landing, putting toilet rolls in the Babbings' en suite and swabbing down the kitchen, all jobs which he would NEVER usually do unless Pinkie-Sue had threatened him with all sorts of unspeakable punishments.

"Housework is fun," he'd said, brushing dog hair from the warm spot in front of the fire. "I don't know what the

Pink Mumma was always complaining about." He frowned. "Do we have a scrubbing brush? I want to do the front steps."

"You can't clean this place back into life," said Miranda testily.

"At least I'm not gadding around like you," said Jackie. "Now leave me alone, woman. I've got work to do."

Miranda felt she had lost all sense of time, but it must be around six o'clock in the evening. A couple were walking their dog on the beach. These were the Watsons. They owned a holiday cottage a few miles away and came down most weekends. The couple halted on the beach and looked at The Dodo Hotel. They were probably wondering why there was smoke coming out of the chimney and the front door wasn't boarded up any more. If they saw her, they'd ask questions. Miranda hid until they'd climbed up the far waterfall path and vanished before she slid from her stone into the sea, swimming out to the deep water. There were no seals anywhere, which was odd; they would usually be basking on the rocks below the headland in this weather. Maybe they were all out fishing.

Miranda swam out just beyond the shadow of the cliff. Here was a raised plateau that housed a shelf of seaweed and lots of little fishes. She avoided the water immediately to the left of this shelf, as the current was strong and on a high tide, it could sweep you a mile out to sea. But to the right of the shelf, the tide was gently pulling in, and Miranda kicked off into deeper and deeper water, sometimes surface swimming, but more often skimming along just below the surface. Swimming was so much easier when you didn't have to wear a rubber sparkly tail.

She rose to the surface and lay on her back. The Dodo Hotel bobbed on the beach, and the cliffs rose out of the water. She thought again about the hidden jet ski. Would there be a chance to ride it?

Miranda felt a strange motion in the water below her and she turned over on her stomach. She was hit by sheer terror. Immediately below was an enormous, gaping mouth, big enough to swallow her whole. Fear paralysed her limbs and threatened to sink her. Black eyes watched her emotionlessly as a huge triangular fin broke the surface. Miranda screamed and salt water flooded her throat.

CHAPTER ELEVEN

Basking

Miranda lashed out, her foot striking the huge creature's skin. It felt as solid as a wall. Miranda lunged for the shore. Any second there would be an agonizing tug on her leg or stomach and she'd be dragged under. She swam on and on, swallowing water and coughing, swimming with panicked, flailing strokes. Then she saw the thing just to the right of her. It was SO enormous, the size of a bus, the size of a whale. It must be a Great White to be so big. A man-eater. The great big mouth was still open, a huge white ribbed, gaping mouth.

Without any teeth.

Miranda veered off to the Dummity Rock and clung to the ledge. Gasping, she hauled her body out of the sea as the waves lifted her up and set her down on the lower ledge. When she was clear of the water, she inched round the rock and now, staring down, she saw the vast shadow of the creature.

This was no man-eater. It was a basking shark. Basking sharks didn't eat humans, they ate microscopic sea creatures. Miranda let out a laugh which turned into a sob. The only danger from this thing was if it accidently walloped her with its tail, or crushed her. She watched the massive shape slide through the water, and then a wave broke open as big dark triangular fin pierced the surface and the creature stuck its head right out. It looked like a huge, flat, heaving rock, with flabby flat gills reaching almost to the top of its neck and staring lidless eyes.

"Oh," said Miranda, and they looked at each other. Then the thing flopped away and the water folded in contra currents as the gulls mewled above.

Miranda clung to the Dummity Rock, scouring the sea for a long time until she was sure it had swum away before she slipped reluctantly back into the sea and swam unsteadily to the shore. She took off her fins and crossed the beach, her legs wobbly and a tight feeling in her chest. That had been terrifying and amazing. She had heard of these creatures being spotted around the Cornish beaches before but as far as she knew, one had never been spotted here, in Dummity Bay.

The hotel was empty and quiet. Miranda crept up the stairs to her room, her teeth chattering with cold and nerves.

Her room had the best view of the beach; she could see

the far end of the bay, with the waterfall path snaking up the cliff and at the other end, the dark mouth of Seal Cave. Miranda peered hard at the sea, trying to locate the basking shark. She felt exhausted after her shock and sat heavily on her bed.

Miranda opened her eyes. Something had just crashed to the floor downstairs. She sat up. According to her phone she had been asleep for an hour. She knew Cal and the Babbings were out. So the noise must be Jackie. Or Hugo. She felt a finger of fear. What if it wasn't either? She quietly crossed the carpet, opened the bedroom door and listened. She felt a rush of relief as she heard Jackie chattering away to Fester.

"Don't leave your fleas on their bed. I don't mind fleas, guests do."

Miranda dressed in her stiff, dirty clothes and ran down to join her brother.

"Jackie, Jackie, I saw a shark!"

Later, Cal reappeared with Doris. They staggered in with carrier bags stuffed with food. Doris gave Miranda a hug. She was wearing her green fifties dress with a yellow cardigan and brown lace-ups.

"Do you really have guests or is Cal winding me up?" she asked.

Miranda pointed at Jackie, who was scribbling in the hotel ledger in the window.

"I couldn't turn them away," he protested. "They had cash."

"But they could be anyone," said Doris. "And you're here all alone."

"They're harmless," said Jackie. "Mr Babbing told me he used to be a doctor before he retired. So we're actually safer now they are here."

"They must be suspicious about the lack of adults," said Doris hotly.

"Have you told anyone about us?" Jackie pointed his pen at her.

"No," Doris replied. "But this deception is, like, way out of my comfort zone. What if something happens?"

"It's all right, Dorrie, I'm here," said Cal magnificently.

"Not here all the time," said Miranda in a small voice, remembering earlier when she thought they had intruders.

"Hold your line," said Cal, looking at Miranda. "Don't bail out on me."

"How much are eggs?" asked Jackie, returning to the ledger.

"Depends if you go for battery or free range," said Doris, brightening.

"Which is cheaper?" asked Jackie.

"Do you really not know?" Doris was the only one who was surprised. Jackie had never before been interested in household matters.

"Free range is much kinder to the chickens. Battery chickens have no room to move, but their eggs are cheaper," explained Miranda.

"Then battery it is; we're on a tight budget," said Jackie. "How much is bacon?"

"Organic from the butcher or mass-produced from the supermarket?" asked Doris.

"What time are the Babbings back?" interrupted Cal.

"They've gone out to dinner," said Jackie. "They'll be back late."

Cal looked shifty. "Only the tide is turning, and I've got a spare board . . . we could cook later. . ."

Some things never changed.

"Watch out for the shark," said Miranda.

"What shark?" asked Cal, his eyes lighting up.

Miranda explained.

"Holy moly! It might still be there. I got to get out there!" Cal ran out of the room, dragging Doris with him.

"Not the usual response when a large shark is found in shallow waters," observed Jackie, twisting his pen in his hair and securing a topknot.

"It would be unusual for us to be usual," said Miranda.

A little later Miranda added some garlic to her vegetable stew. They were coping, though admittedly the stew looked rather watery, and the tinned spinach Cal had brought home had turned the whole thing a nasty shade of green.

What if they got a few more guests, and earned just enough money to stay here? This was their second night, and nothing really bad had happened.

How long could they remain here? No one regularly came here to swim, apart from Doris and Cal's surfing friends, and they were all back at school or college. Most people visited Ayran Bay, a mile round the corner, which was bigger and much easier to find, or Belieze, which had flat golden sands, a large car park, a handy little jetty and a loo. Not many people bothered to come down to their tiny beach, accessed only by narrow winding lanes before you even reached the cliff car park. It always amazed her, that on the most glorious August day, Belieze Beach would have holidaymakers queuing out of the car park, with barely any space to sit on the beach, but just a mile away, their own bay would be deserted.

The stew was smelling odd. She gave it a stir. It could sit for half an hour or so. She could go for a swim if she wanted but she didn't fancy it with the basking shark being out there. She hadn't recovered from the shock yet, and her hair took ages to dry because it was so long and the one thing Pinkie-Sue had taken with her was the hair dryer.

Miranda wandered through the dining room and into the reception. She winked at Hugo, still in his frame above the desk. Pinkie-Sue hadn't packed him because she said he belonged here. Miranda ran a finger over the fine sand which had blown in through the gaps in the window frame, luxuriating in being here, at home.

She found Jackie's ledger on the counter.

Eggs £2.40
Bread for two days £3.50
Bacon £2.50
Tomatoes free from garden
Mushrooms, £3.00 TOO EXPENSIVE
PROBLEMS
HOW CAN WE GET MORE STUPID GUESTS?

HOW DO YOU WASH SHEETS? (ASK DORIS)
WHAT IF THEY WANT AN EVENING MEAL?
WHAT IF THEY WANT BOOZE? (ALL
UNDERAGE, EVEN CAL) (THOUGH HE
LOOKS NINETEEN THE WAZZOCK COS OF
HIS CHEST HAIR)

Miranda was laughing over this when she heard the back
ship door slam and footsteps running through the hall.

"What is it?" asked Miranda as Jackie burst, wild-eyed,
through the swinging doors.

"Holy cow," screamed Jackie. "The police are coming
down The Nip."

CHAPTER TWELVE

In The Devil's Pudding

Miranda closed the kitchen window, then raced round to reception and, with trembling fingers, locked and bolted the front door and turned off the lights. Luckily, the sitting-room fire had gone out hours ago.

"Do we hide outside or in?" asked Jackie.

Miranda thought. "Outside, in case Fester woofs."

They hurried down the hallway and out to the garden, locking the ship's door behind them.

Miranda pulled her spare swimsuit and towel from the washing line, then they all crawled under the bushes at the base of the cliff just as two police officers walked into the garden.

Miranda was shaking and Jackie had sickly green tinges round his mouth.

"Are they going to take us away?" he whispered.

They heard a thump on the door.

"No sign of forced entry," said a male voice. Miranda and Jackie fell silent. That was PC Oliver Trewanny. He was an ex-surfer champion. He and Cal got on very well. All the same, Jackie clamped his hand over Fester's muzzle.

"Some of the windows have had boards removed but none are broken," the policeman said.

"I can smell food," said a female officer. She had a harsh, grating voice, like metal being dragged over a road. Miranda made a face. This was PC Dellard. She was the elder sister of Morag, the chief mermaid, and she was twice as terrifying.

"It's bound to be another false alarm," said Oliver Trewanny. "You know how hyper Neighbourhood Watch are round here."

"Cornwall is plagued by squatters," said Dellard darkly. She cleared her throat. "You knew the MacNamara family, didn't you?"

"Yes," said Oliver. "Good people."

"They've run down this place," muttered Dellard.

Jackie growled and Miranda touched his arm.

"Hippies," said Dellard. "They had no idea how to run a respectable business."

"Hotels are closing all over Cornwall," protested Oliver. Miranda smiled. Good old Olly.

Dellard only grunted. "The children were wild," she said. "I'm glad they're off my patch. I know they'll be trouble when they're older. Especially that girl, Miranda.

She attacked my little sister recently. Nearly drowned her in the mermaid tank."

Miranda's mouth fell open in disbelief.

"That doesn't sound like Miranda," said Olly. He cleared his throat. "This place won't be the same without them."

"I expect some of their hippy friends have broken in," muttered Dellard. "I'm going to look round the front."

When the two were out of sight, Miranda pointed to an overgrown, roped-off path cut into the cliff.

"Move."

This tiny path, directly behind the hotel, was out of bounds to everyone. It was overgrown with brambles and ferns and in places vanished altogether. The children were forbidden to come up here because rocks would sporadically tumble from the lip of the cliff above. The path led to a fissure in the granite which opened out into a deep network of caves. Creeping up through a tunnel of bracken and weeds, the children climbed into the curve of the cliff, only pausing now and again to look down to check the police had not returned. The narrow opening of the cave was about a quarter of the way up. Miranda hesitated under a fall of ivy. The cave entrance was only a few metres up but heavy loose rocks lay on the ledge above it where they had fallen away from the clifftop.

"If one rock lands on your head you're dead," Cormac had said.

Miranda looked up at the vast rock formation above her, then at Jackie's curly head and Fester's wild mop.

What was she doing risking all their lives?

"We have to go back," she whispered, though the last thing she wanted to do was face Morag's sister.

"Never," said Jackie and plunged in through the ivy, Fester scrabbling behind him.

Miranda felt a sheen of sweat on her skin. She really, really didn't want to arrive at her new school in a police car. Hearing the crunch of shoes on the stones below, she hurried after Jackie into the darkness.

The moment she entered the cave the temperature plummeted and the chill stroked her skin. There was a damp, close feel to the air, like nothing had moved in here for hundreds of years. She felt her way along the rocky, cold wall, moving her feet slowly over the oddly smooth slabs below. She tried to remember the last time she had been in this cave. It was maybe three years ago. She, Cal and Jackie hadn't gone far before they'd heard footsteps behind them, and torchlight, and Cormac had appeared in the darkness.

"You're NOT allowed to wander in here. Pinkie is going crazy down there." But then he'd come with them, and shown them various openings and tunnels, and pointed out a large hole in the ground, deep in the cliff, which, he said, led to the Seal Cave. Miranda thought about this hole now, and toed the ground nervously. If she fell in she'd land right on the jet ski.

"Be careful, Jackie," she called into the void.

"Oh chill out," Jackie replied from somewhere. "Me and Fester know these caves like the back of our paws."

"How come?"

Jackie didn't answer.

Miranda edged forward. How long would they have to wait in here before the police went away? She gave a little shriek as something grabbed her arm.

"Only me, knobbly knees," said Jackie. "Come on, you're taking ages."

He pulled her forward. The tunnel widened and there was a crack in the rocky roof above. It grew wider and ferns and mosses and damp plants of all sorts started appearing. Then the roof opened out completely and the children found themselves out in the open at the bottom of a giant, grassy bowl. This was known as The Devil's Pudding.

"Shall we get out here?" Miranda didn't want to go back into the darkness.

"No, stupid. When they drive back along the cliff road, they'll see us."

Jackie dragged Fester back. The place was thick with rabbits and the dog was getting amped, as Cal would say. They fell back into the darkness, their footsteps echoing.

"I wonder who called in the cops?" said Jackie.

Miranda didn't answer. It could have been anyone – a tourist, a local, maybe even someone who knew them.

"They're on to us now," said Jackie gloomily. "We probably ought to run away again, before we're caught and hauled to that school."

"I'm not running anywhere," said Miranda. "We're going to get caught sooner or later." Water dripped from the roof, landing coldly on her neck, like witches' fingers. The tunnel widened and lengthened and as Miranda's eyes adjusted to the darkness she could see stalactites forming on the roof and the dull outline of the rough rocks beneath her. Cormac said that in the past these caves had been used as dwellings, hiding places for smuggled goods and a place where soldiers sheltered and refugees hid.

A few minutes later and they entered a large space, lit with a shaft of light and stretching round in a broad circle. There was a wide pool of clear water in the centre. A thick blanket of ferns covered one wall, starting brown and shrivelled at the bottom and growing green and lush nearer the roof, where the sparkles of jade light danced over the rock. The whole place smelled green. Fester padded over and drank noisily from the pool.

"I wonder how deep it is?" Jackie said, picking up a stone and throwing it in. They watched it turn over and over in the clear water before it disappeared into the gloom.

"We could get some scuba gear and go cave diving," said Jackie excitedly. It was typical of him to suggest something that none of them were actually able to do.

Miranda wondered if the police would poke around on the beach. If so, there was a possibility they would find the jet ski. And if that happened, the place would be crawling with people. The children would be discovered very quickly. She thought of Cal and Doris and hoped they had stayed away. Her fingers closed round a smooth rounded rock. Imprinted on the surface was a perfectly preserved image, like a large woodlouse. It was a fossil, a trilobite. It felt funny to think that it had sat here, in this cliff, with no one knowing about it for millions and millions of years until this moment.

"What's this?" said Jackie, now in the corner of the cave.

There was a pile of papers and dried-up chips on the ground. It looked shockingly out of place.

"It must belong to a tramp," said Jackie. "How exciting."

"It's not yours?" asked Miranda uneasily. How horrible to think that someone had been in here and they had known nothing about it.

"I wonder if it has anything to do with Cal," said Jackie.

Miranda didn't think so. Cal, when he wasn't in the cold, wet ocean, liked things to be comfortable. He loved warm fires, a soft chair and hot food. Holing up in a dark, dank cave was not his style.

"Maybe he meets Doris here," said Jackie and winked salaciously.

"I don't think so," said Miranda. She looked nervously round the cave, half expecting some dark figure to step out of the shadows.

Then they both went still. There was a knocking sound coming from the tunnel they'd just come through.

"It's the cops," whispered Jackie. He made to move to the back tunnel but Miranda stopped him. There was a breathy roar washing in from the main tunnel, a booming sound from above, which seemed to travel over their heads.

Maybe it was the vibrations of the police car driving overhead.

The children hurried through out of the cave and along the tunnel to The Devil's Pudding. Blinking in the sunlight, they climbed out of the darkness and up the steep, scrubby slopes. They crept to the brow and peeped over.

"Back," Miranda frantically mouthed at Jackie. The police car had stopped only a few metres away. Miranda gestured for Jackie to lie down but Fester saw a rabbit and whined, straining at his lead.

"Did you just hear something?" PC Dellard's sharp voice rang out.

The children held their breath. In the quiet that followed there was only the clunk and squeak of Hugo's winch as it swung in the breeze.

"I'll take a look," she said. Jackie's eyes widened in horror as Dellard's head and shoulders appeared over the brow of the Pudding. Her bobbed brown hair blew across her face.

"Excuse me." A male voice came from the road. "Can you tell me the way to St Austell?"

Dellard turned away, taking a few paces back down the hill. As she gave clipped directions, the children wriggled back down the Pudding. They heard the sound of car doors slamming and of an engine starting up. Then there was a rush of air as the police drove away.

"That was interesting," said Jackie, gripping Fester's collar. "But I feel a bit sick now."

After a short while, Miranda tentatively edged back up the slope and peeped through the heather. The police car was whisking away down the lane, vanishing into the hedges. And there was the dark silhouette of a tall man, walking quickly. Was it the hiker she'd seen yesterday?

A rabbit broke from a clump of bracken and Fester slipped his lead and charged after it. Jackie followed.

"I think Fester deserves a nice rabbit after all that keeping quiet," he called. "See you later." Th[...] depression and over towards the head[...]

Miranda sat on the rim of the Pudd[...] a boulder, and blew out her cheeks. Sh[...] with relief. Her elbows and knees were coa[...] and she had scratches all up her arms. Gra[...] stopped hammering as she took in the view. T[...]orth the land rose and fell. To the east the sea heaved and twinkled. The sun was vanishing over the cliff and the sky was turning pink. She stuck her head over the boulder. The winding lane threaded down through the familiar landscape of fields, hedges and sheep. The hiker was now just a stickman.

As she watched, he suddenly turned and seemed to look back in her direction. Miranda held still watching him, and a feeling of coldness came over her. Then he turned back and continued down the lane.

Had he seen her? She had no idea.

CHAPTER THIRTEEN

The Awakening
of Pinkie-Sue

Miranda could not sleep. It was now around midnight and she had lain for an hour in the dim light of the moon. There was something knocking on the Circus tower above her and she was trying very hard not to get scared about it. It was bound to be something rational, like a gull, or the wind moving something. Things were always rattling or creaking in this old house. An image of the man on the cliff came into her mind. She couldn't help thinking that he'd been huge, like Hugo. NO! It was the hiker she'd seen. Ghosts didn't ask policewomen for directions. She forced the vision of Hugo with his creepy white eyes out of her head, instead going back over the events of the day. She pictured the gleam of the jet ski, the wide mouth of the basking shark, the arrival of the police and the scramble up to the caves.

She thought again of the figure standing motionless in the road.

The knocking overhead started up once again.

"Oh GO AWAY, Hugo," snapped Miranda. "I don't believe in you."

Cormac's mother, Granny MacNamara, had once told her that if you believe in ghosts, they are much more likely to appear, as they know you are "receptive". It was logical, therefore, that if Miranda didn't believe in Hugo, then he ought to go away. But it was difficult to tell him that you didn't believe in him without his face materializing, his Victorian-suited figure clump, clump, clumping overhead, leaning over the parapet, his ghost dog at his heels. Didn't you have to admit something existed in order not to believe in it?

The puzzle went round and round in Miranda's mind.

At least the Babbings had been no trouble. When they'd arrived back in the early evening, they seemed in an excellent mood.

"No matter," Mrs Babbing had smiled when Miranda had called over to apologize that the chambermaid had been off sick today and their room hadn't been tidied. She was wearing thick orange lipstick and a deep red skirt. Her hair was stiff with spray. "This is an adventure for us, isn't it, Joe?"

"It's like *Fawlty Towers*," said Mr Babbing, and they both burst out laughing.

Miranda didn't know what they were talking about so she had left them to it. Thankfully they didn't ask for any food as they had already eaten, and after a long walk up and down the beach, a short, surprisingly fast swim right across the bay by Mr Babbing and a drink in the bar (served by Cal, who had carried all the booze back in from the outhouse) they'd gone to bed.

Miranda sat up in bed and gazed around her empty, moonlit room. The shark had come and gone; ditto the police. Jackie had even had a bath. This was the third night they had been here, and still no one had discovered them. This was stolen time and she was loving it.

A loud KNOCK KNOCK came from above. Like someone was banging their fist.

Miranda gave up. She got out of bed and put on a large top of Cal's. She cautiously opened her door and looked up the steps leading to the parapet. Everything was empty and still. The knocking had stopped. Miranda swallowed. It was ludicrous to believe in ghosts.

"I'm not scared of you," she said defiantly, her neck prickling. She had grown up with these unexplained disturbances, and the only way to deal with them was to be strong. She padded down the steps, along the landing and then down again to the kitchen. When the hotel was fully operational, the MacNamaras had mainly lived in the family room next to the dining room, but the hotel kitchens, with their wide stainless-steel tables, big metal sinks and white-tiled floor, had become the new place to hang out.

Miranda took the laptop from the shelf, powered it up and switched to her email. She got a little shock when she saw there was a message from her mother, sent only a minute before. Miranda felt a tug of longing for Pinkie-Sue.

She read the email.

DEAR CAL, MIRANDA AND JACKIE.

WHY HAVEN'T YOU RUNG US? MY MOBILE NUMBER SHOULD WORK OR USE THE HOTEL NUMBER AT THE BOTTOM OF THE PAGE. WE ARE DESPERATE TO HEAR HOW YOU ARE GETTING ON.

JACKIE?????

WHY HAS CAL TURNED OFF HIS PHONE? WHY DON'T YOU ANSWER YOURS? IS THERE NO SIGNAL AT YOUR SCHOOL EITHER??? EVERYONE SAYS HELLO AND WISHES YOU WERE HERE.

WE HAD SOME STRANGE NEWS THIS MORNING. SOMEONE CONTACTED THE ESTATE AGENTS AND TOLD THEM THE DODO WAS NOT FOR SALE!

WE CAN'T THINK WHO WOULD DO SUCH A THING. WE ARE VERY BUSY TODAY BUT AS SOON AS WE CAN WE HAVE TO INSTRUCT THEM TO SELL IT ALL OVER AGAIN. WHAT A PAIN. THEY ARE BEING VERY SNIFFY ABOUT IT. I SPOKE TO AUNTY, WHO SAID SHE HAS NOT HEARD FROM YOU EITHER.

IF I DON'T GET A CALL SOON I AM GOING TO DEFY THAT RIDICULOUS SCHOOL POLICY AND

RING THE HEADMASTER AND DEMAND TO SPEAK
TO YOU!

TALK SOON, OR SKYPE, OR AT LEAST EMAIL
ME BACK AS SOON AS YOU GET THIS MESSAGE!

LOVE PINK MUMMA AND BOOK DAD XXXXXX

Miranda chewed her thumbnail and decided to send a second
holding email until she'd had a chance to talk to her brothers.

HELLO! WE'RE OK. SORRY WE HAVEN'T RUNG.
WE MISS YOU TOO. JACKIE IS VERY HAPPY AND I
AM GRADUALLY SETTLING IN.

WE HAVE MET SOME NEW PEOPLE. DON'T
WORRY ABOUT US.

LOVE MIRANDA XXX

A few moments later the laptop gave an annoying little
ping. She had a new message.

Miranda raised her bleary eyes to the screen and bit her
lip. It was another message from Pinkie-Sue.

Subject: WHAT ARE YOU DOING UP?

MIRANDA? IT MUST BE MIDNIGHT IN THE UK?
WHY AREN'T YOU IN BED? DOES THIS SCHOOL
ALLOW YOU TO ROAM THE INTERNET IN THE
MIDDLE OF THE NIGHT? CAN'T YOU SLEEP? ARE
YOU UNHAPPY? I THOUGHT YOU WERE IN A
DORMITORY WITH THREE OTHER GIRLS. AREN'T
YOU KEEPING THEM AWAKE?

DARLING, WHY ARE YOU AWAKE? IS
EVERYTHING OK? THINGS SEEM ODD. GO TO
BED NOW OR YOU WON'T HAVE A NICE DAY
TOMORROW. LET'S SKYPE TOMORROW.
LOVE FROM YOUR WORRIED MUMMA XXX

Hell! Miranda had completely forgotten about timings. She cursed her foolishness.

MUMMA! RELAX! I JUST COULDN'T SLEEP AND
WAS LOOKING FOR AN EMAIL FROM YOU, WE'RE
CONNECTED! I AM IN MY OWN ROOM, IT IS VERY
NICE. I'LL GO TO BED NOW, EVERYONE THINKS
I AM ASLEEP. CHILL OUT. WILL TALK TO MY
TEACHER ABOUT SKYPE.
LOVE MIRANDA XXX ZZZZ

She hadn't really told any lies, not huge ones anyway. Maybe she should have come clean now, but she didn't want to alarm them. If Pinkie-Sue and Cormac knew what their children were doing, they'd be back on the plane straight away.

The laptop pinged again. It was yet another message.

OK, I FEEL A BIT BETTER. NOW GO TO BED. I'LL
SPEAK TO YOU ALL TOMORROW WITHOUT FAIL
LOVE MUMMA XXX

Pinkie-Sue mustn't Skype tomorrow. How would they pull it off? Miranda switched the machine off and began the ascent to her bedroom. There was a light on in the Babbings' room which she hadn't noticed on the way down, and she could hear low murmuring. After a lifetime living with guests, she knew that many more people were awake in the dead of night than one might suppose.

She paused at her door, wondering if she dared step up to the turret and breathe some night air, but another knock from above sent her scuttling into her room and locking the door.

The sun was streaming in her window and from outside Miranda could hear the seagulls screeching and the tide washing high on the beach. She sat up with a start. There were cooking sounds and smells wafting up from the kitchen.

She might have missed the Babbings' breakfast!

She rapidly dressed in yesterday's clothes and scurried downstairs. She heard the concierge bell and raced along the corridor into reception in time to catch the Babbings just walking out of the door.

"I . . . is everything all right?" stammered Miranda.

"No one was around so we thought we'd slip away. Your grandmother made us a cup of tea first thing." Mr Babbing rubbed his stomach, which was straining against a white and blue flowery shirt. "She said breakfast was never before nine a.m. out of season."

"My grandmother?" Miranda stood stock-still. As far as she knew, Granny Lamarque was with her parents in America, and after that on to Mauritius, and Granny

MacNamara was holed up on the west coast of Ireland.

"I was beginning to think there were no real adults here at all!" laughed Mrs Babbing. "I thought your big brother was in charge."

"Oh, we all pitch in," smiled Miranda. Grandmother? What grandmother? Was Aunty Mad here?

"You are a credit to children everywhere," smiled Mrs Babbing, once again revealing her terribly white teeth. She jangled her gold bracelets. "Everyone is always saying how awful the youth of today are, but you're practically running the place!"

"We're all a team here," said Miranda.

"Doesn't it affect your schoolwork?" Mrs Babbing asked, pushing a stiff wing of sprayed hair back on her head and fixing it with a lethal-looking hairpin.

"We're homeschooled," said Miranda quickly.

"This place is ever so old, isn't it?" warbled Mrs Babbing. "I'd love to have a bit of a stickybeak in the other rooms before we go."

"Sorry," said Miranda. "They're not available for viewing."

Mrs Babbing sighed. "Ah well, I'm just a nosey nosey, aren't I?"

"We're off to pastures new," said Mr Babbing before Miranda could agree. "We're all paid up."

Miranda asked if they wanted their luggage winched up the cliff.

"Such service!" laughed Mrs Babbing. "No, sweetie-pie, with my handsome hunk of a husband we'll be up in a jiffy!" She took Miranda's wrist. "Will your father be coming back from his rest anytime soon?"

"Soonish," smiled Miranda. She said goodbye to the Babbings and fled before they asked her any more awkward questions.

She found Cal cooking bacon and eggs in the kitchen.

"Cal, they said Aunty was here!" said Miranda.

"False info," said Cal, and pointed to the corner of the room, where an elderly figure sat hunched over her breakfast. She raised a fork and pointed it at Miranda.

"*Metten daa*," she said.

CHAPTER FOURTEEN

Mrs Garroway

"*Daa lowar o ve*, Mrs Garroway," exclaimed Miranda. "I'm OK." She grimaced at Cal, who shrugged and turned back to his frying pan.

"You're not supposed to be here!" Mrs Garroway rubbed her chin.

Miranda smiled weakly. "Well, no . . . but. . ."

"Where are Mr and Mrs MacNamara?" asked Mrs Garroway.

There was a long silence.

"I see." The old lady folded her arms. "A load of gockies, int you?"

"What's that?" asked Miranda.

"Look it up," said Mrs Garroway irritably. She always got cross when the children didn't understand Cornish.

"We won't be here very long," said Cal.

"No, I don't suppose you will." She rummaged in a plastic bag at her feet and slapped two large silvery fish, pollocks, on the counter behind her. "You'll be wanting these, I expect."

Mrs Garroway kept her small boat, the *Mary-Joy*, in the tiny bay below her house, and used to supply The Dodo and many other local hotels with fresh fish.

"*Meur ras*," stammered Miranda. "Thanks." The old woman nodded and turned her attention back to her breakfast.

Miranda stood close to her brother, who was dropping the last sausage into a frying pan.

"What now?" she whispered, glancing at the formidable old woman in the corner.

Cal shrugged.

"But this means it's all over, surely?"

"Only if she tells," said Cal. "And you keep forgetting I'm sixteen. I'm legally allowed to look after you two."

"*Badna mouy tay?*" called the old lady. "And I wouldn't mind more hog's pudding. Get goin' on the hedges after."

"She wants more tea and sausages," said Miranda, interpreting. She'd learned a bit of Cornish at school. "After that she wants to trim the hedge."

"That's what I said," said Mrs Garroway primly. "*Pa pynjay.*" She made a squawking noise and flapped her arms.

Miranda was fairly sure she was being called a parrot.

"Er, we can't afford to pay you for the gardening," she said awkwardly.

"I'm not abandoning my garden. *Tabm mouy bara?*" said

Mrs Garroway. "A bit more bread, please."

"On the double," said Cal. "How did you know we were here?"

Mrs Garroway looked at him in disbelief. "Everyone knows you're here!"

"Who's everyone?" Miranda gripped the edge of the counter.

"Everyone in the pub, anyway. You got smoke coming out your chimney. You got Callum headin' up to the cafe for his chips. You got yourselves playing on the beach. The word is you never left."

"Oh," said Miranda, abashed. She thought they had remained hidden.

"You'll be dragged back to your school soon enough, I daresay. In the meantime I would like some tomato ketchup."

"You mean, you won't tell?" said Miranda.

"Tell who?"

Miranda shrugged.

"I already told the police, course I have," said Mrs Garroway. "I told them they should come down here and sort you out." She tsked. "Fat lot of good that did. They think I'm a mad old gockie anyhow. They didn't even believe me at first. I had to insist they came. I said if you children came to harm it would be their fault."

"That was you who called the police?" Miranda felt betrayed.

"Course I did," snapped the woman. "I'm up there in my house twitching about it."

Cal drew himself up to his full height. He cleared his throat.

"Mrs G. Don't worry at all. I am nearly seventeen and I am the head honcho here. I am legally entitled to look after my siblings. You can tell that to anyone who asks."

"Ha," said Mrs Garroway. "Messing about at night. . ."

"What?" Miranda turned to her brother, who looked blank.

Mrs Garroway put egg in her mouth. Then she set about eating the rest of her breakfast and everyone knew better than to interrupt her.

This was all startling information. Miranda busied herself making toast with the last of the bread, wondering how it was going to change things. The door swished and Jackie wandered in with Fester at his heels. He was wearing a pair of grubby shorts and a too-small T-shirt. Yesterday's suit lay in a damp huddle outside the back door. He was sockless, shoeless and he had a big yellow spot on his chin. He came to a standstill when he saw Mrs Garroway and Fester bumped into the back of his legs.

"Huh?" he said, pointing at her.

"Scarf this, brah," said Cal, handing Jackie a steaming plate of food before he could say anything rude.

For the next five minutes everyone concentrated on their breakfast. Cal had fried the eggs to perfection, the sausages were crispy yet tender, the bacon was good; even the beans tasted fantastic.

Miranda wiped her toast around her plate, soaking

114

up the last juices from the grilled tomatoes. The food was making her feel better. They would sort this out, somehow.

"Er, Mrs Garroway, are you intending to tell the police about us again?" she ventured.

"I'm not. But someone else might. How long are you planning to stay, anyway?" asked the old woman, pushing her plate away.

"Not much longer," said Cal. "Another day or two at the most."

Mrs Garroway nodded. "You'd better take your brother and sister back to the school by the weekend or I'll drag you to the police station myself. And mind you tell your mother where you are. I'm going to be keeping a close eye on you."

"Sure thing," said Cal. They all watched as Mrs Garroway rose.

"Hedges spittin' berries," she said, leaving the room by the back door. A few minutes later they heard the *clack clack* of her hedge clippers.

"She said everyone knows about us," Miranda noted. She caught sight of her laptop lying next to Mrs Garroway's fish and remembered Pinkie-Sue's emails.

"Boys," she said. "There's another problem. Pinkie wants to Skype us."

"I'll email her and tell her the school don't do Skype," said Cal. He sighed.

"Lies, lies."

The bell in reception rang.

"You go," Miranda ordered Jackie. "Maybe the Babbings

115

came back."

"No way," said Jackie. "I'm a werewolf at breakfast. I need the food to go down before I turn human."

"I'll go," said Cal. He turned when he reached the door.

"Guys, we've got to get cooking on our exit plan today." The doors swung shut behind him.

Two minutes later he was back.

"Kind of an issue here," he said. "We've got another guest. It's a scientist dude."

For a few moments, everyone was silent. Miranda stared at Cal.

"A new guest?" Her voice was shrill. Could they get away with it twice?

"Make him pay a cash deposit," urged Jackie.

"Tell him we're full," said Miranda. "I don't want any more strangers here at night now we're on our own."

"You know I'll always look after you," said Cal, and Miranda smiled. Cal always said the right thing. He checked the door was shut behind him and stepped into the room.

"He says he doesn't want any meals and that he'll be out all day and most of the evenings. He only wants a bed for two nights. The Babbings have left, so we could cope."

"He can go in the Yellow Room," said Jackie.

"The Babbings were in the Yellow Room," protested Miranda.

"Good," said Jackie. "That means it will be clean and tidy for him. What's his name?"

"Red Hodson," said Cal. He rubbed his ear, something

he did when he was worried. With his orange flowered shorts, his black hair falling over his shoulders and turquoise T-shirt bringing out his green-blue eyes, Miranda thought he looked extremely handsome. "Look, guys. I'm wondering if we should call it a day. We've had a ball here, but things seem to be hotting up."

"SHUT UP," howled Jackie. "We can't give up now. We've been here for THREE nights and it's been AMAZING. If you turn us in, Cal, I'll, I'll KILL YOU and Fester will BITE your corpse."

"Oh flip," murmured Miranda.

Then, to the children's utter horror, a strange man poked his head in through the double doors.

"Hello," he said, a little self-conscious. "I heard shouting. Is everything all right? Are you full of guests?"

Everyone stiffened. No guest was EVER permitted to come into the kitchens. This was sacrosanct. This man had crossed the line. He was about thirty years old, thin and of a medium height with very dark hair cropped close to his head. He had a triangular-shaped sternum, so his chest poked out like a bony bird. His forehead was criss-crossed with worry lines and his left thumbnail was black, like he'd hit it with a hammer.

"Sorry," said Miranda stiffly. "Guests are not permitted in here." She'd recognized him at once. He was the hiker man who had been hanging around.

"Oh good, I am a guest," smiled the man. "I'm desperate, you see."

Miranda couldn't place his accent. It was north country

117

but also a little bit French.

He had a friendly, twinkly sort of face, despite the lines, and wore knee-length shorts and one of those vest-style jackets with a million pockets, each one stuffed with pens and maps and torches and bits and pieces.

"Could you wait outside?" asked Miranda in a high voice. "We won't be a minute."

"Of course." The man vanished and the door swung closed. Miranda couldn't help noticing the eggshells scattering the counters left over from the massive breakfast and hoped the man hadn't seen them.

The man popped his head around the door again. "I really will be no bother. I've been camping but it looks like the weather is on the turn. I'll be easier than your other guests. I'm a scientist, researching cliff erosion and coastal ecosystems. . ."

"We will be with you in ONE MINUTE," thundered Miranda.

The door shut again and Jackie went to stand in front of it.

"He seems harmless," he said. Nobody replied.

Miranda scooped up the eggshells and threw them in the sink.

"Arrrrrghhh," she said. "What a dilemma! The money would be nice but I'd rather not have the hassle."

"I can tell him no," said Cal. He glanced at Miranda. "I think we're coming to an end here anyway."

"I don't want any more grown-ups here," said Miranda. "They only complicate things." She sighed. They seemed to have more guests turning up now The Dodo was closed than when it was open.

"I'm with you, dude," Cal replied. "I'll go out and sort it."

"Show no mercy," said Miranda. "Right, Jackie? Jackie?"

But Jackie had slipped away unobserved. Fester remained, wagging his tail under the central table, making the oven trays rattle and spoons wobble. They found Jackie sitting on the desk in reception and writing slowly and laboriously in the ledger.

"Booked," he said with a satisfied smile.

CHAPTER FiFTEEN

Betrayal

Red Hodson had taken possession of the Babbings' old room. Jackie said he had already accepted the money and he couldn't renege on the deal.

"I DID tell him that we were likely to go out of business any day, and that he had to pay every day." Jackie smiled winningly at his siblings.

"How long does he want to stay?" Miranda asked.

"He said as long as he could," said Jackie.

"You've really done it this time," said Cal. "I thought the general vibe was we were leaving tomorrow."

"Today," said Miranda. "But everyone is always saying time doesn't exist here."

"You might be, but I'm not." Jackie folded his arms. "No one is making me go to that school of fools who are trapped behind the wall."

Now Miranda sat on the beach in the sun, trickling the sand between her fingers. She was wearing her wetsuit and flippers and was getting ready to swim out to find Mica. She watched their new guest as he negotiated The Nip, binoculars to his eyes. He'd told them again that he was a scientist, and that he was from the University of Aberdeen, but was doing research at Plymouth. Then he'd unloaded bags and cases and flight cases and padded folders and wallets and files from his car (a five-year-old gold Nissan with bronze-coloured wheel trims) and winched them all down the cliff himself.

Doris sat on the sand next to Miranda. She had turned up at lunchtime, laden with bags full of apples and crisps (for the children) and bread, ketchup and soap (for the new guest).

"My mother asked if I knew anything about a rumour going round that the MacNamara children had run away back to The Dodo," she said.

Miranda screwed up her mouth. "So we're really busted?"

"I said, 'Sure, Ma, I'm off to see them now,'" Doris smiled. "She didn't believe me, of course, but my conscience is clear. I told her the truth."

She rolled on to her stomach and looked at Miranda. "So what are you guys planning to do? Cal is being a bit, you know, cagey."

"We have no plan," said Miranda. "I'm going to watch over the seal pup. Otherwise we're just kind of bumbling along."

"Good luck with that," said Doris. She watched Red pick something up and scrutinize it. "He seems chilled."

Miranda shrugged. "The Babbings were completely lame, but this one is more switched on. Any minute he'll complain about the dirty room, or the lack of food, or no booze, or room service, or clean towels, or anything, and he'll ask to see the manager, and then we're DOOMED."

"Cal could pass himself off as the manager any day," said Doris dreamily.

It was a warm, sunny day, far too hot for the end of September. A tourist family with three small children were paddling in the shallows. Miranda gazed at the bright sea and the golden sand, at the grey-brown cliffs and the water marks in the sand. Why did she feel like she was sleepwalking through the days? And Jackie was completely out of control, or as out of control as a ten-year-old could be whilst simultaneously planning the breakfast menu.

"Come on," said Doris, picking up her surfboard. "I'll race you in."

Miranda got to her feet, waddled over the beach and waded in up to her waist, gasping at the cold. She dived, shivering as the water engulfed her; then she swam hard out to sea, following Doris's expert strokes. After a while Miranda turned and floated on her back. Red had vanished from The Nip. Hopefully he would be gone for the rest of the day.

"There's Cal, see you later," said Doris, and kicked off to join him.

Miranda waved at Cal, who was far out to sea, beyond

The Teeth. These jagged rocks were well known to local sailors. Several vessels had sunk on this stretch of water. The deadly rocks occurred on a rise in deep water, and they were a major reason why only local sailors and fishermen ventured into this bay. If you were a good swimmer you could dive down, and at the bottom of the sea was a fishing boat from the 1940s, and next to it lay the rotting hull of something much, much older. Miranda had several souvenirs from these wrecks (now locked in suitcases in storage) – a bone china cup, in perfect condition, with pink roses round the rim, and also the remains of a metal knife. It was part of her plan to one day do a proper dive down there, with breathing apparatus, and see what else she could salvage. Miranda swam for Dummity Rock, slightly more nervous than usual, and keeping her eyes open for any large gaping-mouthed shapes in the water. But the basking shark must have gone to a different bay. She climbed on to her ledge for a rest. She could see Pasty and Grandma sunning themselves on the rocks. They were so fat they looked like grey rolls of blubber.

Miranda combed through her hair with her fingers. She thought, as she had done many times before, that from a distance she might be mistaken for a real mermaid, not a crazy one with a sparkly tail and breathing tube in the glass aquarium at MYRMAID WYRLD. Her hair was a mess. It had been so long since she had brushed it there were dreadlocks forming at the nape of her neck. There was also an unpleasant tingle on her scalp. Miranda picked through her hair. She hoped she didn't have nits.

And then she saw a head bob up in the water. Mica! The pup eyed her, then vanished. A few seconds later she popped up much closer.

"Hello," said Miranda. "I hope you've been catching fish."

The pup twitched her whiskers. She looked darker, older than even a day ago.

A movement on the headland caught Miranda's eye. She stood to get a better view and Mica dipped away. A figure dressed in red charged hell for leather along the precipice, followed by a brown shape, and then darted into the bracken. Miranda frowned. What was Jackie up to now?

Then she saw. A yellow Mini was parking in the cliff car park, sending seagulls screeching into the air.

There was only one person who drove like that. Someone who had passed their driving test fifty years ago.

Aunty Mad had come to The Dodo Hotel.

Miranda plunged back into the sea, making for the corner of the beach.

The Whale Stone stood in a few centimetres of water. Miranda crouched behind it as Doris and Cal slithered over to join her, carrying their surfboards under their arms.

"You saw her, then?" panted Cal.

Miranda nodded. A strand of seaweed had got caught in her mouth. She spat it out.

"We have a situation," said Cal. He crawled up the rock and peered over at the beach.

"She's poking around outside The Dodo," he reported. "Now she's looking in through the dining room window. Now she's trying the door. Thank God it's locked. Anyone know where The Scientist is?"

"We saw him on The Nip about a quarter of an hour ago," said Doris.

Cal rubbed his chin. "She's going into the back garden. Where's Jackie?"

Miranda told them she had seen him on the headland.

"Cal, maybe you should just go and find her, and tell her what has happened," said Doris.

Cal rubbed his nose. "I can't face her," he said. "I was hoping we could sort this out without involving her. She'll lose the plot."

"She will," nodded Miranda miserably. She shivered. The sun had gone behind a cloud.

"I had hoped we could just kind of arrive at the school and take it from there," said Cal.

"I've said I'll take Fester," said Doris. "Mum has always said she wanted a guard dog." Miranda knew Fester would be a useless guard dog as he adored all humans, but it was a relief to hear that Doris would take him. She'd be a better owner than Aunty Mad.

"But why is she here?" Miranda asked. "Why is she poking around?"

"She's just checking the place over," said Cal.

"Or looking for us," said Miranda. "Maybe Mrs Garroway told her too."

"Oh dear," said Doris. "She's coming down to the beach."

Miranda scrambled up the slippery rock and gazed over the top. Aunty Mad was dressed in brown, her favourite colour. She was carrying her stick and what looked like a mobile phone, which she was holding close to her ear.

"No signal," murmured Cal.

Aunty walked along the pebbles at the top of the beach, searching the cliffs. Then she made straight for their hiding place.

"She knows we're here, she knows!" Miranda jumped up and down with nerves.

"Reckon we can swim round to Mrs Garroway's bay?" Cal looked at the sea. The tide was going out. It was possible to swim round, but it was on the borderline between exciting and stupid as the water was deep, and the currents could take you quite far out. Also, if the three of them did attempt the swim, they would be visible from the headland above.

"Actually, I don't think we should," said Cal, glancing at Miranda. "But I don't want to be caught here like a little kid."

Doris patted his shoulder. "She might be worried about you," she said. "Maybe we should just face the music. What's the worst that can happen? A little shouting?"

A shrill whistling filled the air.

"I know what she's doing here," said Miranda. "She's not looking for us. If she thought we were missing, the place would be thick with police cars. It's not us she's after, it's Fester. Maybe she thinks he found his way home."

Cal slapped her back. "You're right. OK. That changes things." He pointed at the Seal Cave behind them, the place they'd hidden the jet ski. "We can sneak in there, then climb up through to the caves above."

Keeping low, the children wove through the rocks and

crept inside the cave.

To Miranda's surprise, the jet ski no longer had a plastic wrapper on its seat and it had a swirl of seaweed stuck in its rudder. The trailer wheels were thick with damp sand. There was also a strong smell of petrol. Two life jackets dangled from the handles.

"Cal?" Miranda flicked a dead crab from the footings. She could feel a slow anger building up in her.

Cal looked sheepish. "I only took it out once, or twice," he said, unable to look at her. "I couldn't resist it."

"When?" asked Miranda, swallowing.

Cal hesitated. "I didn't want Jackie to see, so I had to take it out at night." He coughed. "I couldn't stop myself. Miranda, *ma soeur*, all this running-away business is stressful. I've had to take responsibility for you all. Going out at night on this, skimming the waves at high speed, it's been awesome. Just the rip I needed."

"You didn't take me!" Miranda clenched her hands into fists.

"Sorry, babe, I. . ."

"And you left me and Jackie alone at night?" Miranda's voice echoed back at her.

"You had Fester," said Cal. "And I was only out for a little while."

"You left us alone with the Babbings!" hissed Miranda. "They could have been axe murderers, or child abductors. How COULD you, Cal?" She felt the weight of tears behind her eyes.

Cal looked miserable. "Betty, babe — everyone was

127

asleep."

"Traitor," said Miranda. She turned away. Cal was trying to round her by using his pet name for her.

"We'd better start climbing," said Doris gently. "Your aunty is nearly here."

Miranda refused to take Cal's hand as he tried to help her up through the crevice in the roof; the way into the upper caves. She shrugged him off and pulled herself up the slope, scattering loose stones, kicking sand and grazing her knee. To think that Cal, lovely Cal, her big brother could be so mean. It was bad enough that he had abandoned them, but what was much worse was being left out. She was dying to ride the jet ski.

The next few moments all got rather difficult and stressful. It had been a long time since Miranda had attempted this climb and it was not easy barefoot. Cal had swarmed up first, in order to help the others, and he kept kicking dust and stones into Miranda's face. By now she was so cross she wanted to run out and see Aunty Mad and tell her everything.

"You left me alone with Hugo," panted Miranda.

"I'm grovelling here," said Cal. "I couldn't help myself, and anyway you don't believe in the guy."

Once in the upper cave, the three of them sat in silence in the darkness, catching their breath. One tunnel ran right to the cliff edge; the other joined up with the caves Jackie and Miranda had been hiding in the day before.

"Doris," demanded Miranda. "Did you know Cal had been going out at night and leaving us?"

Doris made a ticking noise with her tongue. "I didn't

know you had the jet ski until I heard Cal banging on my window on Monday night," she said. "He'd come round the bay on it."

"It was a bright moon," said Cal dreamily. "The water was black and as still as a millpond."

"I had a ride in my pyjamas!" said Doris.

"Bully for you," muttered Miranda.

"It was the best night of my life," said Doris, and she rubbed her nose on Cal's cheek.

Miranda bit her lip. "A midnight sea ride would have been the best night of my life too," she said, and stormed off into the darkness.

CHAPTER SIXTEEN

The Wire in the Cave

Miranda felt her way along the tunnel. It was getting easier to see where she was going. The floor sloped gently and in the centre there was a narrow groove which ran with water. She felt annoyed rather than angry with Cal. Did the fact that he had been taking it out at night, and riding it, mean that her brother was a criminal? Cal was always so kind and thoughtful, and dependable and trustworthy. But after this, she felt she didn't know her brother at all. What else had he been up to behind her back?

She hurried on towards the ledge, where the tunnel opened out in the middle of the cliff, like a balcony. Here she would have a good view of the beach. Golden shafts of sunlight struck the far wall and mosses and grasses were growing in the crevices of the rock. And there was something else. Miranda noticed a thin black line, like electrical cord, running taut along the face of the rock. Startled, Miranda touched it with one finger. Yes, it was electric wire, like the lead for a computer.

What was it doing here? Miranda looked round into the darkness, remembering the food wrappings she and Jackie had found in the other cave.

Feeling jittery, Miranda followed the wire down the tunnel, stepping as quietly as she could through the gloom.

Miranda blinked as she stepped into the light. The ledge jutted out two metres or more over the cliff, with the sea churning below, throwing up foam as it hit the rocks. There was a curved roof, maybe eight feet high, and the floor had been worn smooth and was padded with sand coughed up from the churning sea below.

Miranda found it hard to believe what she was seeing. The wire led to a small metal table and stool, perched upon which was some kind of box-shaped electronic device covered with clear plastic sheeting. The table was tucked behind a rock and under the roof of the cave so everything was quite dry. There was also a large black plastic crate, the sort used for recycling, padded with bubble wrap and containing a small square switchboard, with three fat dials down the side and rows of silver switches and a microphone. Miranda glanced over her shoulder, frightened that whoever this stuff belonged to would come back. There was also a box containing a sleeping bag, a small gas stove, some pans, some freeze-dried food and a bottle of milk. It must belong to Red.

He'd said he'd been camping, but why did he need all this electronic stuff?

Miranda unfolded a piece of paper which was resting on the table. It was a printout of all the tide times and the Coastguard stations of the English Channel. There was also a map of the south-west coast, weighed down with pebbles. It gave her a nasty shock to see that their own little Dummity Bay had been circled in red pen. It was all very unsettling. Miranda put everything back and looked out over the cliff ledge. There was no sign of Aunty Mad on the beach or on the far cliff. Miranda felt her way back through the tunnel and found Cal and Doris skimming stones over the pool in the Fern Cave.

"Am I forgiven?" asked Cal, giving her a winning smile.

"Come and look at this." Miranda took Doris's hand and led her back to the cliff ledge. Cal followed.

"Whoa!" Cal undid the bubble wrap and examined the stuff inside. "It's a CB radio. And this," he held up a chart, "is a map of the shipping lanes."

"I know, I know," said Miranda crossly. She gave him a sly look. "Don't even think about stealing it."

Cal frowned. "Miranda, I. . ."

"What do we do?" interrupted Miranda. "It's creepy."

"I don't like the vibe either, babe," said Cal. He reached up the wall. Hidden in a crevice was a large silver-wrapped package. Cal carefully uncovered a large white dish, the size of a small tabletop, with wires and spokes in the centre like the plug of a light bulb.

"Satellite dish," said Doris.

"Back up, girls. Stay out of sight." Cal pointed to a figure walking on the far beach under the waterfall path.

"That's Red," said Miranda. "I think all this is his."

Red was now unlatching a theodolite and positioning it on the beach.

"You don't think this has anything to do with the jet ski, do you?" asked Doris. "Maybe he's looking for it. How much are those things worth, anyway?"

"He might not be a scientist; he might be a police detective." Cal rubbed his chin nervously. "What to do? What to do?"

Doris was looking at the black wire. "Where does this go?"

"I don't know," said Miranda. What she said next surprised everyone, including herself. "I'm going to find Aunty and I'm going with her. I've had enough and I'm taking Jackie. Cal, you can do what you like."

"I don't think the little chick has forgiven me," Cal remarked to Doris.

"Oh, go for a jet ski," snapped Miranda. She wished he would take her seriously. She rushed back into the dark tunnel, palming the damp walls to the Fern Cave and The Devil's Pudding.

But when she pulled herself out of the Pudding and on to the cliff, she saw the back of Aunty Mad's Mini as it sped down the lane.

"Aunty!" shrieked Miranda. "Come back! We're here." She waved and jumped but the Mini kept going. And at the crossroads, it turned right.

"LOOK IN YOUR MIRROR!" howled Miranda, but Mad wasn't stopping, and in an instant she had gone.

"I HATE THIS," yelled Miranda.

"What's wrong? I thought this is what you all wanted?" Miranda jumped as the strong old figure of Mrs Garroway suddenly materialized behind her. She was carrying a stick and wore her green headscarf wrapped tight round her head.

"*Fatla genes?*"

"I'm OK," said Miranda gloomily.

"You lot give me the earache. Put this on." The old woman gave Miranda her jacket. Miranda wrinkled up her nose. The jacket swamped her. It was brown tweed and stank of old woman's armpits. Miranda put it on all the same, and felt a mixture of relief at the sudden warmth and revulsion at the sour smell.

"*Meur ras,*" she said.

Mrs Garroway eyed her. "Time to move on?"

Miranda looked away. "I guess so."

"Phoned Mrs MacNamara yet?"

Miranda shook her head.

Mrs Garroway reached out and gripped Miranda's shoulder with her strong, gnarled fingers.

"Do it now. Then pack up, catch the bus, and get yourself off to your school," said Mrs Garroway, staring right into her eyes. Her voice rose. "There'll be a great fuss and everyone will be jumping around, but you got to face up. You could catch a train tonight. Turn up on the doorstep. They won't turn you children away."

"The boys won't want to come," said Miranda.

Mrs Garroway looked down at the beach and frowned. "Who is this new fella? The lad wandering around in short trousers?"

"That's a scientist. Red Hodson," said Miranda. "He's staying at the hotel."

"He has strong legs for a scientist," observed Mrs Garroway. "Otherwise I don't like the look of him. Send him packing." She tugged a lock of Miranda's hair. "Go tonight," she urged. "Before you get into real trouble. Something's up. Don't know what. But it is." She nodded and stomped off through the thrift grass. She turned round. "If you're still here come morning, I'll drown the lot of you."

She shook her head and continued to walk. "COMERO WEETH," she shouted without looking behind her.

"You took care of us when you ratted on us to the police. . ." muttered Miranda. The gulls were wheeling in the breeze, and a golden aircraft split the sky with its smoke trails. Miranda turned and ran as fast as she could in no shoes, over the cliff to The Nip and back down to The Dodo.

By the time she got there her feet were scratched and sore and she had a splinter in her big toe. There was no sign of The Scientist, or Jackie and Fester. And when had she last seen her little brother?

She ran round to the back of the hotel and let herself in. She stepped on to the carpet. She felt full of a new resolve. They would tell Red he had to leave, then pack their bags and clear out. They also needed to ring Pinkie at some point, but first they had to work out their story.

Miranda had a quick shower so she wouldn't look too awful when she turned up at school. Then she went downstairs into the hotel kitchen. It was deserted, and the morning's breakfast dishes sat greasily in the sink. A trail of muddy paw prints led across the floor and five or so fat blue and black flies buzzed around the overflowing bin. She felt hungry so she opened the fridge and eyed Mrs Garroway's fish. Maybe Cal would cook them before they left. It would be a shame to waste them.

She jumped as the phone began to ring. Miranda looked at the number on the screen. The first digits were +001.

America!

The answer machine clicked in.

"*Hello, this is Pinkie-Sue. Your mother. Cal, are you there? The school say you didn't turn up. Aunty says you might be here. Miranda? Miranda? Pick up right now. MIRANDA. JACKIE. PICK UP THE PHONE. I'M GOING TO CALL THE POLICE IF I DON'T HEAR FROM YOU!*"

"WHERE IS EVERYONE?" howled Miranda. They hadn't agreed what to say yet.

There was a clatter from under the table and Miranda clutched herself in alarm. She stepped back as a head poked out.

"Has Mad gone yet?" Jackie whispered hoarsely. "She's been poking around outside."

Fester crept out on his belly.

"*ANSWER THE PHONE*," screamed their mother.

"I have to," said Miranda, moving towards the phone.

"Don't, she's bluffing," said Jackie. He rushed over to

136

Miranda and held on to her waist, dragging her away from the telephone. "She doesn't know we're here."

"GET OFF ME," screamed Miranda, elbowing her brother in the face. "I have to answer."

"*I KNOW YOU ARE THERE. WE'RE COMING BACK RIGHT NOW,*" howled her mother.

Miranda grabbed the receiver.

"Mum?"

But the line went dead.

CHAPTER SEVENTEEN

Red's True Colours

"So we're all packed?" Cal was rubbing wax into his surfboard with a tea towel.

Miranda nodded. Her bags were piled up behind the desk in reception. She and Cal were sitting on the large bench outside the hotel, wedged between a topiary shark and a pot of lavender, watching Jackie and Fester run in and out of the waves. Doris had gone home. She said her mother was suspicious about where she was spending all her time.

When Cal had come in from the cave, he had listened to Pinkie-Sue's anguished message on the machine and had held up his hands.

"OK, we're through."

They decided they couldn't face Pinkie-Sue live on the

phone, instead sending her what Cal called "a mother-block email".

Dear Parents,
    We messed up, especially Cal. But we are all fine and are going to put it right. We have now left The Dodo for good and are staying the night with friends. We will arrive at the school tomorrow (can you let them know?).
    Please don't worry. Cal is looking after us.
    We are sorry,
    Cal, Miranda and Jackie.

"Why did you say we were staying with friends?" asked Miranda.

"Because otherwise she'd send Mad around again," said Cal. "We'll stay one more night, then fly out of here in the morning."

"It won't fool her," said Miranda. "So you're going to tell The Scientist to pack his things?" She spoke quietly, unsure of the whereabouts of their unwanted guest.

"Sure," said Cal. "I'll ask him to quit. It's pretty aggro, though."

"Cal, we can't have guests here," said Miranda. "We're closed. We'll say Jackie made a mistake."

Miranda thought Cal was only agreeing to this because he felt guilty about his jet ski adventures. She looked at her watch. It was six-thirty and she wanted her dinner. She wanted Pinkie-Sue's cooking. She wanted vegetable samosas, chicken creole and chickpea bread, with a heap of steaming aromatic rice. She did not want any more stale bread with peanut butter and she would never be able to eat another bacon sandwich.

"Cal, about the pollock. . ."

A shadow fell over them.

Red. He must have come from round the side of the house. He was wearing sunglasses and had big sweat patches under his arms. She wondered how much he had heard.

"Lots of fossils in those rocks," he said. He hesitated, took a mobile phone out of one of his many pockets and checked something on the screen.

"No signal," muttered Miranda.

"You kids are having some kind of adventure, aren't you?" he said, putting the phone away. He regarded Cal buffing up his board. "Where are all the adults? Do you actually have any other guests? I thought there was an old couple staying here."

"S'quiet season," said Cal.

Red looked across the bay, then studied the hotel, scrutinizing the fences and the boarded upper windows.

"Where are your parents?" he asked.

"Flying," answered Cal vaguely.

"Fly fishing," interrupted Miranda, glowering at Cal. Why should they tell Red their business?

"Really?"

"Down the bay," said Miranda. She was fed up with all of these questions. She wanted some answers of her own. "What's all the stuff in the cave for?" she demanded. "All the machines and maps?" Cal gave her a warning look.

Red frowned. "Not mine. What sort of machines?"

Miranda looked at Cal. If the stuff didn't belong to Red, then whose was it? Whatever the case, if her brother wasn't going to get rid of this man, then she was. The sooner they were shot of him, the better.

"I'm afraid we are going to have to ask you to leave." She felt her face burning. "Unexpected complications have made it impossible for us to accommodate you this evening. Our brother should never have let you have the room. We can give you the number of an excellent hotel in the village."

There, she'd done it. She was quite proud of that speech. It sounded very grown up. But Red didn't reply.

"We'll give you a full refund," continued Miranda, hoping Jackie hadn't been up to the cafe and blown all of Red's cash.

More silence. Cal was screwing up his toes in his flip-flops and Red seemed very tall against the sky.

"That's impossible," he said lightly. "I've paid for tonight. I'll be gone first thing."

Miranda and Cal exchanged a pained look.

"Dude – I mean, Mr Hodson. I'm afraid my sister is correct. We're, like, closed," said Cal. "Sorry, man. We're in over our heads here. We can't do the hospitality thing tonight. We're probably leaving the hotel tonight ourselves."

"Really?" The Scientist looked startled, but then he collected himself. "Then I can stay here on my own."

"No, man." Cal stood, but Red cracked his fingers and smiled a sudden, nasty smile which transformed his face.

141

"So who is going to make me go?" he said.

Miranda was taken aback. "Sorry?"

"I know about you kids," Red said softly. "One call to the police and you'll spend the night in a cell. I've seen the stolen jet ski and I know you are runaways."

For a minute no one said anything. The sea just washed in and out, in and out, the same as ever. But everything was different.

"Easy, man," said Cal, pulling himself together. He seemed smaller and younger than usual. "We're only discussing bed and breakfast."

"Good," said Red. "We'll have a quiet night tonight and I'll be gone first thing in the morning." There was a heavy silence. Miranda was unable to look at him. This was all going wrong. She felt her mouth go dry.

"I think the maximum term for unlawful marine looting is fifteen years," said Red brightly. "Customs officials hate smugglers, even immature ones."

Miranda was speechless. This was horrible. Everything had changed.

"I won't be needing breakfast," said Red. He lowered himself to the beach and strode off over the sand.

CHAPTER EiGHTEEN

The Shadow in The Circus

The MacNamara children sat on the blowy cliff, just beyond The Devil's Pudding. The sea slapped into the rocks below. They watched as their newest guest walked up and down the remaining strip of beach, his binoculars trained on the horizon. It was eight o'clock in the evening, and getting gloomy. The tide had pulled right in and there was a line of clouds building on the horizon.

"We've got to scram, people," said Cal miserably. "This Scientist guy is, like, unpredictable."

A helicopter crossed the sea, miles away from the land. It flew like an angry fly in the darkening sky.

"Search and rescue," said Jackie, pulling his faded towelling dressing gown around him. It was his only clean outer-garment. "I can tell by the chugga-chugga. They train most Wednesdays." He wiped his nose on the sleeve.

Was it really Wednesday? Since they had come back to The Dodo, Miranda had lost all sense of the days. She watched as a large black beetle crawled through the long grass on the very edge of the cliff.

"Guys," said Cal. "Are you listening? We're in a situation here."

"More information required," said Jackie. "Where are we going to go?"

"Aunty Mad," said Cal. His voice softened. "Or over to Doris's."

"But I don't like Doris's mum," said Jackie. "Her toilet flushes green water." He took a pasty out of his dressing-gown pocket and stuffed a corner into his mouth.

"Where'd you get that?" asked Miranda, her stomach lurching in hunger. It had been a long time since Cal's wonderful cooked breakfast.

"I stole it from the waste-paper basket in The Scientist's room," said Jackie, stuffing more into his mouth. Miranda watched as he had a coughing fit. "You should see the stuff he's got in there," he spluttered. He coughed some more and tears ran down his face.

"Death pasty," said Jackie, when he'd recovered. "Tasty, though."

"You shouldn't go in his room, brah," said Cal. "It's seriously lacking in manners."

"I was delivering the complimentary coffee sachets," said Jackie innocently. "He's got maps, a radio transmitter, loads of phones and a wallet with wads of foreign money inside."

The children observed Red climbing the waterfall path at the far end of the beach.

"So is this Scientist guy our enemy?" asked Jackie.

"Yeah, bud," said Cal bleakly. "The grom snaked me."

Miranda felt scared. If Cal thought there was a problem then things must be bad. "Are you worried about the jet ski?" she asked gently.

"What jet ski?" asked Jackie, pulling the hood of his dressing gown over his head.

"Too right," said Cal, ignoring his brother. "I'm in deep."

"So do we call Aunty Mad?" said Miranda.

Cal drummed his fingers. "The thing is, if Mad comes here, the Red Scientist won't be able to stay and he'll rat on us about the jet ski."

"What jet ski?" repeated Jackie.

"He's horrible," said Miranda. "He's blackmailing us."

"Want me to put a hex on him?" asked Jackie.

"He'll be gone come the dawn patrol," said Cal. But he looked worried.

"You hope," said Miranda.

"Let's go now," said Jackie, jumping up. "Let's get a bus, get a train and GO TO SCHOOOOOOL." He wheeled about, arms outstretched.

"You've changed your tune," said Miranda in astonishment.

"The food is rubbish here, I've had enough," said Jackie. "I'll never grow into a man on the slop you've been feeding

145

me. I keep thinking about all the blackberry and apple pies I'm missing."

"What about Fester?" asked Miranda.

"Oh, I'll sneak him in," said Jackie nonchalantly.

Miranda didn't doubt it. "What about The Wall of Discipline?"

"I like a challenge."

"The issue is, we've bailed on the bus," interrupted Cal. "The next one isn't until eight in the morning."

"All right, we'll get that one," Miranda agreed. A herring gull wavered in the air above them and landed on the ground just a few feet away. It eyed the remains of Jackie's pasty.

"Beat it, sea rat," shouted Jackie, and the bird took off.

"Dudes, lock your doors tonight," said Cal. "This guy is low." He lowered his voice to a whisper, though there was no one around. "I know what to do. I want us all to leave dead early, OK? When Red is zonked out, I'll come and get you. We can get up The Nip and go and hike down to the main road."

"Why sneak out?" Miranda was confused. "Why not just leave?"

Cal seemed to be struggling with something. "Look, I don't want to scare you guys, but I just don't like The Scientist. I don't trust him. Regular citizens don't talk like him." He scratched his neck. "I don't want him to know where we are going."

"So we're just running away?" said Miranda. She felt

sure Cal was making this more dramatic than it needed to be. Cal frowned. "I just think it would be shrewd to get out of here."

"We're double runaways," said Jackie. "Cool."

"We should eat, then hit the hay," said Cal. "It's late. I'll wake you guys at like five in the morning. Wait for me to come to you."

"I'll just go and say goodbye to Mica," said Miranda.

Cal looked worried. "No," he said. "That grom is down there. I want you both to hang with me this evening." He pointed at Miranda. "I'll cook you that fish, swirl up some chips and we'll have us some farewell chow."

He touched Miranda's nose.

"Don't worry, Betty, everything is going to be all right."

Miranda opened her eyes. She had no idea what time it was. Outside it was very dark and the moon had been wiped out by the clouds. She could hear the night wind skittering over the sand.

Someone was talking somewhere in the hotel. In the quiet of the night it sounded very loud. It was a man's deep voice, firing out words in a language she didn't recognize. Miranda sat up, taking care not to make the bed springs squeak. Red's room was down a flight of steps and along the landing. She wondered who he was talking to and how was he doing it without a mobile signal? He sounded angry and nervous. Miranda felt her skin begin to creep. Something was wrong. She slid out of bed and quietly opened the door.

She jumped as there was a loud bang, like someone had

thumped the wall. Then Red shouted, "NO NO NO."

Miranda stepped back into her room and shut the door. She glanced through her window at the dark, rushing sea and shivered. Then she saw a pale light zooming over the water and felt a rush of anger.

Cal! How could he? He'd promised not to leave them on their own again, especially now. But from the look of it he was out there again, riding the jet ski.

Miranda spun round as she heard her door click open.

She clutched her dressing table as a shadow slipped into the room.

"Hugo?"

CHAPTER NiNETEEN

The Lost Boy

"No such thing as ghosts, bud."

Miranda let out her breath. It was only Cal. He put his finger to his lips. There was a longish pause in the talking downstairs before it started up again. Was Red talking in French? Miranda was quite good at the language as Pinkie-Sue spoke it fluently, and she recognized a few words, like *bateaux* and *mer*, but most of it was unclear.

"A few issues going down," whispered Cal. He was fully dressed in shorts, a sweatshirt and trainers.

"I thought you were out there." Miranda, keeping her voice low, pointed to the window.

Cal shook his head. "We should have left earlier." He faced her, his face shadowed. "I just saw torchlight in the outhouse, about ten minutes ago. Then I heard some kind of motor craft and saw lights on the shore. The boat went out to sea."

Miranda swallowed. She felt fear prickling on her neck. "I saw that too."

"I think Red is part of a criminal gang. I found this in the restaurant. He must have dropped it earlier."

Cal passed her a small booklet. Miranda flicked on a pen torch she'd found earlier to examine it. It was a passport. Inside was a picture of Red.

"Look at it closely," urged Cal.

Miranda shone the thin beam of pink light on to the passport. Red looked younger than now, with longer hair and bushy sideburns. Then she clamped her hand to her mouth.

Sampson B. Cartwright

"Spooky, huh?" said Cal, taking back the passport. "What kind of good guy goes by a fake name?"

Miranda thought. "Batman?"

Cal ran his fingers through his hair, worrying at a knot. "I wish he wasn't here," he said. "I don't trust him. I don't think he's a scientist at all. I showed him a marlin skull earlier and the guy thought it came from a sea turtle."

The talking stopped downstairs. Then they heard someone open a door. Footsteps crossed the landing and paused at the steps leading up to the turret and Miranda's room.

Brother and sister stared at each other, appalled.

One second, two seconds, three seconds passed. Red cleared his throat quietly. Miranda was so frightened she wanted to scream. In the gloom, Cal winked at her as they heard the footsteps softly tread the landing away from the turret. There was a series of long creaks as they stepped up to Cal's door.

"Locked," whispered Cal. The children did not move as the footsteps then creaked over the landing to the far door – Jackie's room. Miranda did not want that man going in her little brother's room.

"Fester will wake up," she said. Red evidently thought the same and after a moment he moved on again.

The children listened as he walked down the stairs. There was a series of doors being opened and closed. Only someone who had lived all their life in the house would have heard his movements. But Miranda recognized every squeak and creak. There was the whine of the split door between the stairs and the hall. Here was the crack of the rotten floorboard in the hallway. There was the knocking as he leaned too heavily on the loose balustrade. And here was the soft push of the front door. She heard his feet land in the sand.

The children ran to Miranda's other window, following the beam of torchlight as Red hurried up The Nip. After a few minutes car headlights glared out over the cliff. The car reversed, and vanished into the night.

"Come on," said Cal. "We've got to wake Jackie, and then we have to get out of here. I don't know what this is but I don't want us involved. Get dressed."

He left the room and Miranda hurriedly pulled on her clothes. She picked up her torch. Her bag was already packed downstairs.

She met Cal on the landing and swung the light on his face.

"Jackie's not in his bed," he said hoarsely. "Neither is Fester."

Miranda's heart began to race. "Oh, where is he?" At the bottom of the stairs she automatically went to switch on the light but Cal caught her hand.

"Let's stay below the radar," he said.

As they stepped into the dark, quiet reception, Miranda felt wobbly with fear.

"The little dude always turns up," said Cal, though he didn't sound too sure of himself. "He's probably in the kitchen, raiding the fridge."

He wasn't.

"Maybe he's sleeping in another bed?" suggested Miranda. Last year Jackie had made a habit of sleeping in every empty guestroom so they never knew where they might find him in the morning.

"I'll go and check."

"Keep the lights off," said Cal. "And don't shine the torch at the window. I'll search down here."

Miranda raced upstairs. "Jackie?" she called in a low voice. "Where are you?"

She looked everywhere, even tentatively trying Red's door (it was locked). She poked her head up in the attic and shone the torch through the cobwebs and boxes of jam jars.

She looked in each bedroom, each with a stripped bed and dust sheets on the furniture; she checked the bathrooms, the small sitting room at the end of the landing, and the cleaning cupboard (it was warm in there and was a favourite haunt of Fester's). She looked under her parents' bed and in all the big wardrobes. No Jackie, no Fester. She raced up the steps to the turret and burst out into the night. There was a faint half moon and cloud shadows played over the stone floor. The Dodo flag flapped and rippled, but there was no one up here.

On the lower floor she checked Jackie's bedroom again. He used to have a mound of toys piled up against one wall. Jackie never liked throwing things away, and in this dune he had baby rattles, soft balls, old dolls, countless pictures and scribbles done over the years by all three children, scraps of material, a thousand little pieces of plastic which he swore were all, without exception, an important component of some toy. There were clothes he had grown out of but didn't want to give to the charity shop, string, tennis rackets, football boots, bits of net, shells and driftwood. Pinkie-Sue had given up the endless battles to get him to sort it out. Now, of course, the room was bare apart from a few bits of rubbish and a scruffy photograph of Pinkie-Sue and Cormac lying on the floor.

Miranda picked up a lone plastic arm, probably wrenched from one of Jackie's action figures in some vast atomic play war.

"Where are you, Jack?" she said softly.

As she came downstairs, she heard the front door rattle, and froze.

"Miranda," called Cal.

"Yes?"

"Come here." The normally calm Cal sounded panicky.

Miranda fled down the remaining steps, tripping a little on the last tread.

When she righted herself, she found Cal right by her.

"Bad news," he said breathlessly. "All the doors have been locked."

"What?" Miranda felt a pressure rise up in her chest.

"I put all these back this afternoon because I thought we were leaving." Cal waved at the boarded-up lower windows. "Which means we can't get out of the ground-floor windows."

"All of the doors are locked?"

"Every one," said Cal. "Locked from the outside. And I can't find my keys anywhere. Do you have yours?"

Miranda looked on the hook under the reception table where she kept her keys. They weren't there. *Don't panic*, she told herself. *We'll work this out.*

"We could make a rope and climb out of the top windows," said Cal. "It's not that far."

"We should call the police," said Miranda.

Cal made a face. "Look at this." He held up a telephone. The wire trailed to the ground and the ends had been severed, leaving bare wire.

"We've been cut off," said Cal.

CHAPTER TWENTY

SOS

Miranda suddenly felt angry. How dare a guest do this to them?

"I'm not just waiting here. We've got to get out and get help."

Cal examined the phone. "If I could find a screwdriver and some wire, I might be able to fix this," he said.

Miranda wondered at how calm her brother was. Personally, she felt like screaming.

"I'm going to run all over the house again and look for Jackie and for a way out," she said.

Cal knelt to inspect the phone socket. "You know what Jackie's like. He'll be hiding out somewhere. And I think there's an emergency ladder under one of the guest beds."

Miranda knew Cal was just placating her. She had a deep-niggling fear that Jackie was in real trouble. Back upstairs, she searched through all the rooms a second time, before returning to her own for another jumper. She opened her window. A squall of rain blew in and wetted her face and she shivered all the way down her back. The sea and the cliffs loomed blackly against the dark-blue sky. Miranda looked down to the ground below.

If she jumped out, she would hurt herself; it was maybe fifteen feet to the ground. She would have to climb on to the sill, then lower herself down and drop to the boarding below. Then she'd have to scramble over on to one of Mrs Garroway's topiary sharks. It felt like a wave was turning in her head, and the floor seemed to roll with it. Miranda steadied herself against the sill.

She noticed a distant light out to sea, well beyond The Teeth. It was an orange glow which was blinking on and off, on and off. Off, off, on. She watched, leaned forward, focusing on the light. She watched and a fresh dread crawled up her neck. Flick, flick, flick, then a long light.

Miranda stood very still, not wanting to believe this. She knew what these lights meant. This was Morse code. And the message, winking out over the bay, was an SOS.

Save Our Souls.

Miranda watched. The signal had changed. First there was a flicker, then three long pauses of light. Miranda wrote J on the condensation on the window. Next was a simple flicker, then a pause.

A.

Then another combination of lights. Miranda wrote K.

156

Then SOS.

SOS JAK.

"Oh God, Jackie," she whispered. She looked harder and made out faint white lights, close to the orange one. She heard a clattering behind her and put her hand over her mouth to stop herself yelling out.

"It's only me." Cal stepped back into the room. "I've found the escape ladder in the parents' room."

"Look, look at this," interrupted Miranda, pointing to the sea, so horrified she could barely breathe.

"Hey, what's this?" Cal put his arms round his sister. "Dial me in."

Miranda shook as she struggled to get the words out. Bit by bit she explained about the light on the sea, and the Morse code message.

"An SOS from Jackie?" Cal swore. He watched the light. "What have you got yourself mixed up in, brah?"

"Look at the orange light. It seems like it's a long way out, maybe a quarter of a mile off The Teeth," said Miranda. "But it's moving only very slowly, like the boat is drifting."

Cal peered out of the window. "Did you see a boat?"

"Only lights," said Miranda. "And they've faded."

"Could he have gone out on the jet ski?" asked Miranda, trying not to panic.

"He couldn't manage it on his own," replied Cal.

As they watched, the orange light dimmed and then vanished completely.

Cal turned to Miranda. "Do you think he's been kidnapped?"

Miranda held up her hands. "It seems crazy, but look at his message."

"We have to get out of here now," said Cal. He pulled out his phone. "Maybe if we go up on the cliff we can get a signal." He turned back to the window. "I can't see anything at all now. I think there's a fog coming in."

Miranda did up her coat, swallowed and followed Cal out of her room and down the steps to the lower landing. Then she had a thought. "Shouldn't we signal a message back to Jackie?"

"Whoever has got Jackie out there would see our message," said Cal. "Besides, I don't know if I've got a torch powerful enough." He led her back to the bedroom at the very end of the house. It was used primarily as a storeroom and had damp patches all over the back wall, like a giant doily. The carpet smelled sour and the iron bedstead was old and bowed. A ladder was propped against the wall. Cal thumped the damp window, trying to push it open. When the wood gave way, the children manoeuvred the ladder out of the window and lowered it to the ground. Cal had to lean right out of the window to position it properly. He pulled himself back in.

"Come on. We can't waste any more time here." He swarmed over the ledge. "I'll go first, and I'll help you down," he said. "It's easy. Just don't look down." And he was gone.

Miranda leaned over the ledge into the night and again the ground rolled over like a wave. She held on to the side very tight.

"I don't think I can do this," she said. She gripped the ledge so tightly her fingers felt numb.

"You have to, bud," said Cal below her. "We have to get help for Jackie. And if we stay here, Red or whoever might come back for us."

Miranda tentatively swung one leg over the sill, and felt around in the darkness for the top rung. "I can't find it," she cried, panicking. She felt Cal take her ankle and guide her foot on to the rung.

"You're doing great," said Cal. "Now the other one."

Miranda wanted nothing more than to climb back over the sill, back into the house, to creep into her bed, cover herself with her duvet and hide away from all this, warm and snug in her own bed. But she had to go out into the dark and danger. Jackie needed her.

"Here I come," she said, stepping out into the void.

CHAPTER TWENTY-ONE

All at Sea

Miranda was on the ground sooner than she expected. It was far, far worse worrying about climbing down than actually doing it, and thinking about Jackie had overridden the fear.

"Brave!" said Cal. He squeezed her elbow. "Good work, let's go."

And now Cal was running and Miranda was finding it hard to keep up, as he was much faster than her and he had found a better torch. The nearest place where there might be any mobile phone reception was on the cliff ledge. Otherwise they'd have to run up The Nip and then past the headland, then along the road to Mrs Garroway's house. Miranda could hear barking, the noise coming at her out of nowhere.

Fester!

"Sounds like he's shut in the outhouse," said Cal, running up to the building. Miranda tore after him, hoping she'd got muddled with the SOS thing, and they would find Jackie inside. Cal pulled at the door and it swung open. Immediately a big hairy shape bounded out. It was comforting to stroke Fester's rough coat. It made her feel that Jackie might just fall out of the darkness too. Miranda made a fuss of Fester as Cal searched the shack. After just a minute he came out.

"No sign of the little guy," he said, his voice breaking. Miranda felt her insides curdle with worry.

"But some of the storage boxes have been knocked over."

Miranda couldn't think what it meant. Burglars?

"Let's split," said Cal.

Miranda knew the beach well, but she kept tripping and stumbling. The drop to the beach came much sooner than she expected and she nearly tumbled off the edge.

"Miranda, babe, run faster." Cal was tearing down the beach, his torchlight bobbing away from her. After steadying herself, Miranda ran, chasing through the sand with Fester bounding beside her, and jumped the sand river. In her hurry she fell short and soaked her shoes in the cold, fast-flowing water.

"Miranda," shouted Cal. "I'm going to leave you behind if you don't keep up."

The tide was on its way in. The night was dark with fog,

but Miranda could see the grey gleam of the sand and the hulking cliffs ahead.

There was Cal, a black figure running over the beach, his feet pounding the wet, hard sand. Miranda hurried over clumps of wet seaweed and round the mussel beds, and now they were on the rocks.

"Steady," called Cal, shining the torch for her. Miranda felt her way over, her fingers grasping limpets and shell bits, lumps of rough rock and sea pools.

They tumbled into the Seal Cave. The torchlight bounced off the walls and the shadows were long and frightening. The wind sounded through the crevices and hollows, long low notes that sounded like noises from another, unfriendly world. The water dripped all around them and the whole cave smelled musty.

"It's still here," called Cal. "The little dude didn't steal it." He clambered on top of the jet ski, levering himself up into the cave above with his elbows.

"Be careful," Miranda called, thinking of all the equipment in the caves above.

"I'll only be a minute," said Cal.

Then he was gone, the last flickers from his torch melting into the shadows. Miranda listened to the sounds of knocking stones and scrabbling above. Then silence, and Miranda was left with just the weedy light from her torch and Fester.

She felt her way along the cave wall back outside. She couldn't just wait inside in the blackness. It was too awful. She wondered how Jackie was feeling and the fear threatened to tip her over and engulf her. She shook herself.

"This is scary," she said to herself. "But I still need to FUNCTION."

Once outside, she felt a bit better. It wasn't so creepy out here.

"Hey, Betty."

There he was. Cal stood on the high ledge above, his figure outlined against the dark sky, holding his phone aloft.

"Anything?" shouted out Miranda.

"Not yet," called back Cal. "But it's SEARCHING for a signal."

Miranda held her breath. As soon as they got a signal, Cal would be on to the Coastguard and the police, and then a proper search for her little brother could begin.

"ANYTHING?" she yelled again.

"Not yet," shouted back Cal. "Whoa!" he screamed as something fell through the sky and smashed on the rocks below, making Fester bark in surprise.

"That was my phone!" Cal shouted.

"NO," howled Miranda, clawing her way over the rocks to the spot where it fell. "NO NO NO!"

"Where's your phone?" shouted Cal.

"Flat battery," shouted Miranda. The urgency of the situation was making her light-headed. Fester, barking and yapping, wasn't helping.

Cal vanished and Miranda searched the rocks for the phone even though she knew it was a lost cause. It was too dark and she was sure it was broken.

"Fester, shut it," she hissed and the dog, for once, obeyed.

She reviewed their options. The nearest place with a phone was Mrs Garroway's house, but it would take ages to get there in the dark. She looked out to sea and groaned. Beyond the cliff, and shining only dimly, the orange light was back, only now closer and circled by a halo of white lights.

The orange glow was switching on and off. SOS SOS. Then it was plunged into fog.

She noticed torchlight flickering against the walls and floor of the lower cave and rushed in to find her brother pulling the tarpaulin from the jet ski.

"I'm going out there," he said. "I have to see what's happening. You need to run over the cliffs and get help."

"I'm coming with you," said Miranda, picking up a life jacket.

Cal picked up the hitch of the boat trailer. "Miranda. It's seriously too dangerous."

"You can't leave me." Miranda couldn't bear it if she was left behind. "I might get kidnapped too."

"Oh man." Cal looked at her for a second. He seemed to be deliberating. "Help me with this thing."

Together they wheeled the trailer, with the jet ski stationed on top, to the cave mouth.

"Can you see Jackie's signalling?"

"No." Miranda's voice echoed round the cave. "But I think if we head out of the channel and round The Teeth, then bear to east, we'll be close."

Cal was rummaging in a bag which had been tucked in the side of the trailer. He pulled something out. He turned his back on Miranda and took his trousers off and struggled into his wetsuit. He pulled the suit over his chest and zipped up the back.

Cal held up a second wetsuit.

"OK. I can't leave you here," he said. "There might be others. Let's just whizz out and see what we can see. Then we can buzz off to Cary Bay and raise the alarm."

Cary Bay, just around the headland, had a wide beach, a sea wall, and most importantly, a village made up of six houses. Doris lived in one of them. They would get help from here far more quickly than attempting to run along the headland to Mrs Garroway.

"It's Doris's." Cal gave the suit to her. "It will probably fit OK. Hurry." He picked up the hitch and dragged the jet ski out of the cave.

Miranda really, really didn't want to take her clothes off. She shuddered as she undressed and the wind blew on to her back. She pulled up the wetsuit. It was a little too big in the body, and she had to turn up the ankles. She was fastening the life jacket when Cal returned. He reached behind a rock and extracted a big inner tube.

Cal explained, "We tow it behind the jet ski. It's the most amazing fun."

"I'll bet," said Miranda stiffly. Just what else had her brother been getting up to without her realizing? "But why do we need it? The jet ski is built for two," she said, digging her toes in the cold sand beneath her bare feet. She looked beyond the rocks at the night sea and imagined bouncing over it on a rubber tyre.

"We'll need it if we want to bring Jackie back," panted Cal. "Come on, Miranda, if we're going to launch this thing you're going to have to help me. I normally have Doris to help and she's stronger than you."

Miranda gritted her teeth and helped to heave the trailer along over the wet sand. The thick rubber wheels bounced over the ground.

"This is the hard bit," said Cal as they approached the low rocks. "It's much easier to do this at high tide." The tide was halfway up the beach but it wouldn't be at its highest for another hour. Miranda had to pull with all her strength to get the wheels over the rock. She could feel herself getting hot and the water looked a long way off. She might have given up if it wasn't for knowing that Jackie was in danger.

"Doris is much tougher than you," complained Cal.

"She's four years older," Miranda retorted. Her arms felt like they were pulling out of their sockets.

"Come on," said Cal through gritted teeth. "One, two, three, HEAVE."

It wasn't happening.

"We need, like, a ramp," puffed Cal. "Just to get up this bit."

Miranda had a brainwave. "What about a surfboard?"

"In the shed," said Cal. "I'm going to keep trying."

Miranda ran off into the night, her heart pounding. Fester danced on ahead, his body dipping in and out of the torchlight.

In the outhouse she grabbed the first board she could find and lifted it on to her back. She stumbled through the sand river and up over the rocks to Cal.

"Cheers," he said, taking the board. Then he exclaimed, "Miranda, you grom, this is Pearl!"

"I didn't see." Miranda made a face. Pearl was Cal's pride and joy.

"She might break!" said Cal.

"I'll go and get mine," said Miranda.

Cal looked out to sea at the lights and huffed. "No, man, there's no time. Come on, give me a hand."

Together they laid Pearl across the bottom of the rocks, forming a short ramp.

"Here goes, then," said Cal. They heaved and the thick little wheels of the trailer bounced up the surfboard and over the rock.

There was a sharp crack.

"Pearl!" cried Miranda. She looked at the board and saw the end had snapped away where the wheels had slipped.

Cal made a noise in his throat. "Keep going," he said grimly.

From here it was a smooth run down the wet, shining sand. Neither of them said a word until they were right by the water.

"Have you ever been on one of these?" asked Cal, checking Miranda's life jacket was fastened correctly.

"No," said Miranda.

"Ideally we need to drag her in as deep as we can, then climb aboard and take off. We haven't got time to drag the trailer back. We'll just have to abandon it." Cal coughed.

Miranda stepped into the shallows. Fester hung back,

his head cocked, like he was wondering what they were doing. The fog was now thick and they couldn't see much at all beyond the outline of the far cliffs and the headland behind them.

The sea, however, sounded calm.

When the water was over their knees, they dragged the machine from the trailer and it floated in the surf.

"Hop on," said Cal.

Miranda found it fairly easy to get on, though it did wobble, even though Cal was holding on to the other side so she did not tip it up.

She sat on the padded seat and shivered as the water ran over her feet. Then Cal was in front of her, instructing her to put her arms round him and on no account to let go.

"Don't hit The Teeth," ordered Miranda. "I can't see a thing."

"I could steer out of this bay blindfolded," scoffed Cal. "I bet this fog thins when we get offshore. It's, what, four a.m.? It'll be getting light soon." All the same he looked round and adjusted the straps on her life jacket. "Your jacket has got a light and a whistle. Blow it if you wipe out and I'll find you."

Miranda clung tightly to her brother's waist. "What about Fester?"

The dog was sniffing the waves, stalking something only he could see.

"He'll have to stay here," said Cal. "Come on, buddy, it's show time."

"Back soon," called Miranda, blowing the dog a kiss.

Cal revved the ignition and they were off, bouncing over the small waves at a speed that took Miranda's breath away. The spray flew into their faces and behind them the tyre spun and jumped on its long rope. Although The Teeth were submerged and they could easily clear them, Cal made for the deep central channel out of the bay. Miranda knew this was because the currents around The Teeth could be unpredictable, depending upon the strength of the tide. She saw the shadow of Dummity Rock to their right, and knew they were on the right course.

Now they were beyond The Teeth, Cal was shouting something about a light to her, but she couldn't hear over the noise of the engine. She had never been out this deep before. There were strong currents out here. She didn't know how they worked. There was water everywhere, salt water stinging her eyes and blowing into her hair. The spray drenched her almost straight away and the water was night-cold. Miranda shut her eyes and leaned into her brother's back. She couldn't think of anything apart from the need to stay on. She was holding her brother so tightly, she thought her arms might cramp. Her feet felt numb and her toes were curled like a fist. They seemed to be going deeper and deeper into the darkness.

This was madness.

She could see a swell of water banking up ahead of her. This was a broad ocean wave. Where had it come from? The sea hadn't looked at all heavy from the shore. She could feel Cal tense; then for an instant, she saw the orange light again, shining like an eye through the fog. A line of white lights ran beneath it. Then it was gone.

Miranda heard something above the din of the jet ski, a deep roar, like the grinding of a mighty engine.

Miranda gasped as they rose high on the wave, then sloughed down into the trough.

"We're going back," shouted Cal. "Something's chasing us . . . look."

Without warning, a side bender struck them and Miranda felt herself plucked from the seat of the jet ski and thrown into the mighty, endless cold.

CHAPTER TWENTY-TWO

Wipeout

The noise filled her head, the deep booming and the shock of the cold. She was like a stick being tossed around. The waves pulled at her. It felt like she would break. And it was so cold it hurt. She needed to breathe. Miranda kicked and spat and tumbled. Which way was up? There was nothing below her and nothing above her; she was spinning in a void. She coughed and swallowed water. Then she opened her eyes and saw something that was grey, not black. Miranda kicked and kicked and, miraculously, broke the surface. The air deliciously coated her lungs and whipped the salt out of her eyes. Now she was riding a wave and, of course, she had her life jacket on. She could only watch as she was dragged along and she could see the next wave rolling towards her, which would pound her under. Where had these beasts come from? It had been calm when they'd set off.

A bright, bright light shone in her eyes, come from nowhere. But now there was a noise, very close, and something was tugging at her, up into the night sky. Her arms were being pinched and she was deep in a sea valley with hills climbing both sides, and something was pulling at her as if a giant seabird was plucking her out of the cold like a fish.

Her ribs hurt as she was hauled over the side and she lay coughing in the hull of a small motor boat. Something warm was placed on her. She sat up, spitting water, and saw the jet ski turning over and over inside a moonlit wave. Riderless.

Where was Cal?

"Cal?"

"I'm here, save your breath."

Miranda coughed again and it turned into a sob. Her two terrors melted into the blackness, that she would drown and that Cal was lost.

"You totally walked air back then," gasped Cal in admiration. "Then you, like, spun in the keg."

"It's the bow waves, you fool," scolded a voice which Miranda recognized. It was a creaky sort of voice, one which needed oiling. Mrs Garroway leaned over the ship's wheel and glowered at the sea. The tilly lamp swung to and fro, the powerful light shining over the deck.

"I'll turn that off now," said Mrs Garroway. She stepped over and stroked Miranda's head. A light touch, but Miranda shivered because she knew that she must have been in great peril for the cantankerous old woman to touch her head like that.

"You'd be dead if it weren't for the life jacket," said the old woman, touching Miranda's soaked life vest. She was dressed in a long raincoat, with a sou'wester clamped firmly to her head. Her grey hair grizzled out down her back like wet spider webs.

Cal scrabbled over the deck and hugged Miranda.

"I'm so sorry," he said.

"I was nearly with you," shouted Mrs Garroway, water dripping off her nose. "I was seconds away when the wave tipped you off."

"That was you chasing us back then," said Cal. "How was I supposed to know you were friendly?"

"Those things are only for the calm water," snapped Mrs Garroway. "I heard you go out. You stupid boy!"

"It was calm!" shouted Cal. "That wave came from nowhere."

"The wave came from that," pointed Mrs Garroway.

All at once the fog seemed to swirl back and there it was, suddenly huge. A monster. A real sea monster.

Miranda craned her neck upwards to look at this enormous thing that had seemed to come from nowhere. Why was it so QUIET? This vast machine? The biggest ship she had ever seen, the bow looming above them like a nightmare.

"Whoaa," shouted Cal. "Whoaaa, whoaaa."

It was an immense tanker, and they were floundering in

its path, spun round by the currents as it listed sideways and then rolled back. Bright lights shone from it and it stank like old sea: fish, salt, and stale, heavily salted water.

The tanker leaned closer on every wave.

"Are we going to collide?" Miranda shouted. "Why isn't anyone steering it?"

"No engine, no thrust," remarked Mrs Garroway. "Very odd. We ought to be smashed into smithereens by now." She lurched back to the steering unit and expertly accelerated out of the way, out to sea.

"Thank you, Mrs G," shouted Miranda, realizing the old woman had put herself in real danger to rescue them. "You saved us. You're incredible."

"It's headed for The Teeth," yelled Cal over the din.

Miranda stared back at the ship. In the gloom and through the spray she saw the name: *Oscilla Star.* Everyone aboard Mrs Garroway's *Mary-Joy* stared, transfixed. Now the fog was lifting they could see the sheer scale of the ship. There was a deep sound of moving engine parts and the screech of metal.

"It's an oil tanker," shouted Mrs Garroway. "That'll be maybe twenty-thousand dead weight tonnes of ship there."

"Where are the crew?" gasped Cal.

Miranda let out a shout. "Look!"

At the stern of the *Oscilla Star*, a small speedboat was turning. In the ship lights Miranda saw a man hunched over the steering wheel. There was no mistaking the short, dark hair and the stooped shoulders. Miranda knew it was Red. He accelerated away, skimming the waves towards the horizon. Was Jackie with him? Bundled up in the hold?

"What does that mean?" asked Cal, who had also recognized him.

"That's the second boat to come from this ship," said Mrs Garroway. "The first was one of those inflatable high-performance boats. Overloaded it was, full of men. I reckon they've all abandoned ship. Look, I think they've released an anchor, but it's not bedding in. That's why she's drifting in the current."

"Jackie," howled Miranda, and pointed at a tiny porthole high in the bow of the ship. The orange light flicked on and off. Cal and Miranda worked out the signals.

HELP SOS JACK

"We've got to rescue him," said Miranda.

"We must get to Cary Bay and raise the alarm," shouted Cal to Mrs Garroway. "We need the Coastguard and the helicopters and. . ."

"No time," screamed Miranda. "Look, see how it's heading to The Teeth. It might break up. It might spill oil everywhere." In a flash she saw her beach covered in a deadly black film and the body of a dead seal floating in the wash. She pictured Jackie's face.

"I can't put you in danger again," said Cal. "I nearly lost you."

"Look, look," screamed Miranda. The orange light was signalling again.

ALL

"All what?"

ALONE

"ALONE!" screamed Miranda. "COME ON, CAL. If we don't stop the ship it will smash into the rocks, spill oil, or sink with JACKIE on board."

"Or it might explode," noted Mrs Garroway.

"I can't let you on that ship," shouted Cal. "You might die."

"I may as well be dead if anything happens to Jackie," screamed Miranda. "Come on, this is our chance to DO something."

HELP SOS ALL GONE

"Do you know anything about motor ships, Cal?" Mrs Garroway asked.

"I know how to steer a motor boat like this one," said Cal.

"You'd need to get to the bridge, radio the Coastguard and ask for help and directions to steer the ship to safety," said Mrs Garroway. "The Coastguard would have been here by now if that vessel was still transmitting. You need some engine to steer her clear. Either that or drop the bow anchor and stop the drag. At the very least you need to find the AIS satellite receiver and turn it on."

"What?" Miranda couldn't take it all in.

"Automatic Identification System. Transmits position, speed and course. All big ships have to have them."

"You know a lot," said Miranda.

"It was my life for thirty years," said Mrs Garroway.

"Haven't you got a radio?" Cal asked.

"Of course. Not a modern one, though," replied Mrs Garroway. She sniffed. "*Bryw.*"

"Sorry?" Cal looked at Miranda for help.

"Broken," Miranda supplied.

"I keep meaning to get it fixed. Shame this boat is too small to get a line on board." Mrs Garroway was half talking to herself.

"Why aren't the crew working the ship?" howled Cal. "If they couldn't switch the satellite thing on and steer the ship, I'm not going to be able to, am I?"

"Who knows?" said Mrs Garroway. "But it looks like you're the only one to try."

SOS SOS JAKY

Mrs Garroway motored right round the ship to the port side.

All of a sudden, the wind dropped and everything seemed to go quiet, apart from a clattering, clanking sound coming from the tanker, now only fifty feet away. The *Mary-Joy* was balancing on its bow wave.

Mrs Garroway unhooked the sea lamp from the hook, switched it on and shone it at the vast hull. "That's how they all got on."

A steep metal ladder was attached to the side of the tanker. At the top was a well-lit open doorway.

"I can't climb it," said Mrs Garroway. "I'm too old. My hips wouldn't make it."

"But how would we get close without crashing?" asked Miranda.

The tanker was gradually turning round, its bow end headed for The Teeth.

Yet again the red light transmitted.

177

"We've got to do it," said Cal, a break in his voice. "Or at least I have. Jackie is in real danger."

The old woman looked at him. "It's dangerous for you too. But the swell's not so bad. I can pull up alongside. There'll be time for you to make the climb."

"OK," replied Cal.

"What about me?" asked Miranda.

"It's not safe," said Mrs Garroway. She turned to Cal. "Just get on board and radio the Coastguard. And I'll go and get help too."

"Let's get closer," said Cal.

Mrs Garroway said nothing but slowly turned the boat and motored it closer to the stricken ship. As she drove the boat, Miranda noticed her tightening her own life jacket.

The lights from the rear of the tanker shone on the water, turning it an oily black, and night rainbows formed in the gloom.

"She's flying a Russian flag," called Mrs Garroway. "She'll have come from the Black Sea, I'll be bound."

"How do you know?" asked Miranda.

"Because of the oil fields up there," said Mrs Garroway. "She'll be laden with thousands of barrels of oil. Worth a fortune."

They were coming up alongside and the ship was leaning to starboard. At the bottom of the ladder there was a wide step and a couple of handrails. It didn't look so hard. But Miranda knew that if the ship righted itself too quickly, the small boat would be caught up in a side wave and might be tipped over completely. Then Miranda would be back in the swirling ocean.

Mrs Garroway turned her boat round and moved closer in. She slowed right down, intuiting the pace of the rogue ship so they were moving at the same speed. The tyres that hung all around Mrs Garroway's boat made contact with the massive ship with a thud. This was terribly risky. Once the boats were alongside, Miranda could see the sheer scale of the ship, and how different in size they were. She found herself standing on the edge of the boat next to Cal, clinging to *Mary-Joy*'s metal guardrail. The massive iron hull was close enough for her to touch.

Cal waited tensed and ready until the lee fell flat; then he stepped on to the ladder and began to swarm up. Miranda felt the ship draw her in like a magnet. A split second after Cal, she reached for the ladder.

CHAPTER TWENTY-THREE

The *Oscilla Star*

"CRAZY GLOCKIE GIRL," cried Mrs Garroway as she motored away from the huge ship to safety. "Take great care. *Comero weeth*."

Miranda began to climb. The steps were broad and flat and there was a low handrail running up to help her. She saw Cal, above, climbing fast. He looked back at her and swore.

"Hurry," he shouted from what sounded like miles away. Miranda sensed the weight of the ship under her, felt the depth of the sea beneath her, bottomed by awful rocks and whirling currents.

"DON'T THINK," roared Cal. Miranda climbed, hand over hand, pulling herself up higher and higher, and then she saw Cal's anxious face as he grabbed her under the arms

180

and hauled her into the hatch.

"Miranda, you are insane," said Cal, white-faced. Miranda clutched at her stomach. She had been so tense it was beginning to cramp. They were in a bright lobby-like area, clad in steel.

They saw the lights of *Mary-Joy* speed away as Mrs Garroway bounced over the sea towards Cary Bay. Miranda wiped away the tears that were suddenly flowing out of her eyes. Cal got to his feet, took her hand and led her gently away from the awful open door and the dark, heaving sea and Miranda's stomach began to unknot.

Miranda hugged her brother. They'd made it. Now they had to find Jackie.

Still shaken, the pair ventured down a brightly lit metal corridor towards a staircase. The ship smelled sour and stale. Cal silently pointed to a fire map on the wall. They worked out they were on the lower sea deck and needed to cross the ship and climb three staircases in order to reach the bridge. The ship clanked and moaned and the sea thumped against the walls like it was trying to break in.

"What did Mrs G mean about an explosion?" asked Miranda, nervously listening to a deep booming sound.

"Focus on finding Jackie," whispered Cal.

The ship was old and worn, with rust patches in the ceilings and walls. The children groped their way along the handrails and climbed a metal staircase to the next level. Miranda wondered if her little brother was behind every door, and called *Jackie. Jack?* in a low voice. But the orange light had

181

come from near the top of the ship, close to where the bridge ought to be. Miranda felt like she was in a dream as they hurried through the deserted ship, stopping now and again to check a fire map. One corridor looked very much like another but at one point they stepped into a large open room, full of fat pipes and silent machines that Cal said were generators.

They climbed another steep, metal-grilled staircase, pitted with rust. There were portholes to one side, thick with grime, but she could see the sky, now much lighter than the sea. They continued, stopping only to grimace at one another when the booming of the sea got too loud to ignore. Miranda fingered her life jacket. Would it save her a second time if *Oscilla Star* ran on to the rocks?

Cal twisted open a door and they were in a long, narrow room surrounded on three sides by large, smeary tilted windows. There were tables and rows of squat machines, covered with buttons and panels and television monitors. The place smelled of old carpets and cigarettes.

It was the ship's bridge, the control centre of the *Oscilla Star*. Miranda and Cal went to the big central window. The sea rose below them and to the left, the cliffs were coming into view.

"Where's the radio?" asked Cal as a deep grinding noise made the whole ship shudder.

And now there was another noise, a scrabbling. Miranda raced to the back of the room and found a steel door with a wired glass panel. She gasped as a hand suddenly splayed on the glass and turned into a fist.

"LET ME OUT!"

It was a small hand. Miranda whooped.

"It's US, Jackie, it's us." She found the key, just there in the lock. It turned smoothly and Miranda twisted the handle and pulled the door open.

"Ahhha," said Jackie, and they clung on to each other. And then Cal was there and he was hugging them too.

"Ahhh," said Jackie again.

Miranda pulled back and looked at him. He looked small, red-faced and furious, his hair curled madly like the seawater had got into the roots. He was wearing his towelling dressing gown over his green-striped *Joker* pyjamas and wellington boots.

"Where's Fester?" he demanded.

Cal told him Fester was all right. He hugged Jackie again.

"What happened, little dude?"

"I got kidnapped!" he said, obviously still amazed. "I got nabbed on our own beach!" His grubby skin was streaked around the eyes.

Miranda ruffled his hair. "By who? Why were you on the beach?"

Jackie spoke very fast without stopping.

"I snuck out after you lot went to bed. I wanted to find the legendary jet ski. You lowlifes hadn't filled me in, so me and Fester decided to have a hunt. I was walking past the outhouse when someone put their hand over my mouth. It was like in films! I thought it was you guys at first so I didn't fight back. But then it got rough, you know? Fester went nuts and I knew something was up and my head was

183

mashed into this big belly and I saw someone wearing a balaclava come out of the outhouse. It was hard to see much but I swear he had a gun. A towel was thrown over my head so I couldn't see anything after that. I was picked up and chucked over this guy's shoulder. We waded into the sea and I was dumped in a motorboat. Then my hands were tied up; otherwise I'd have jumped overboard." He swallowed. "There were two of them. One of them didn't say anything the whole time but he tied up my hands with Fester's rope."

"Go on," said Miranda, feeling weak with the awfulness of it all.

"They kept radioing some bloke called Vadim. I think he was on the ship already. The engine was really powerful and loud. I'm surprised it didn't wake you guys up. Then there was lots of shouting and I was carried up a ladder like booty. I thought the bloke was going to drop me in the drink. I could tell he was thinking about it. I was dragged along, still towelled up, and I was slammed in here. I managed to get the rope off and I found the lantern."

Jackie paused for breath. "I heard another boat come close, but it was getting foggy. Then there was lots and lots of shouting in different languages and gunshots. Then the noise stopped. I think the engine cut out. It was so quiet it was spooky. A bit later I saw two boats leave the ship, one ten minutes after the other. The first boat was full of youngish blokes. I thought they must be the ones who nabbed me."

"It sounds like a hijack gone wrong," said Cal.

"I never trusted Red from the start," said Miranda.

But Jackie looked at her like she was mad. "It wasn't Red. It was someone else. Red's not fat."

Everyone went quiet as the ship groaned like a huge metal whale. Cal raced back to the control panels and began tracing each different section with his finger.

"So why did Red come out here?" asked Miranda. "We just saw him leaving."

Jackie shrugged. "Maybe he's the mastermind."

"I need, like, a flow chart," said Cal. "I'm seriously confused at what's going on here."

"I got busted and brought here," said Jackie. "I got locked up. There was a fight, lots of shouting. Then the engine died and we started drifting. After that, two motor boats left and then you guys turned up. It's simple."

"Not to me," said Cal. "It's well flaky."

Miranda was looking out of the window. The back end of the boat had now almost spun round completely and the ship was heading, sideways on, towards The Teeth.

"I hope this tanker is double hulled," said Jackie, "or we're going to spill a load of oil on to the beach. This is an oil tanker. I heard them say so."

Cal was examining a console.

"This one might be a radar," he said, pointing at a small scruffy screen. He moved along. "This one could be something to do with pumps. These are a series of light switches. This is an engine dial. This is a computer telling us about the level of ballast. These are navigation machines."

"What are you looking for?" asked Jackie. "I'm starving,

by the way."

"Radio or the Automatic Identifying Satellite thing," said Cal. He looked at Miranda. "If we can't find the radio, we've got to somehow get on a lifeboat." He looked along the row of machines. "This might be it." He was looking at a panel near the centre of the bridge. There was a set of switches, a couple of large dials and a handset. "It's been disabled," said Cal, pointing to a couple of bare wires.

"Can't we fix it?" asked Miranda.

"Electronics are so not my bag," Cal muttered. "You saw my lack of success with the landline at The Dodo."

"I'd have thought we'd be surrounded by helicopters by now," said Jackie.

"Mrs G says they must have switched the satellite receiver off," said Miranda. "Besides, if no one has called for help, how would anyone know we were here?"

"Look at this," said Jackie, pointing to a screen, which showed an outline of the ship's hull. There was a red cross on the lower part and the screen was flashing.

"I wonder what it means," said Cal helplessly.

"Why don't you ask the crew?" said Jackie calmly.

"What?" Miranda and Cal stared at her brother.

"I'm pretty sort of definitely maybe sure they're all locked up down below," he said. "Or some of them, anyway."

CHAPTER TWENTY-FOUR

Prisoner on the Bridge

Miranda had visions of desperate men locked up in a metal prison, with seawater pouring in. She looked back through the open doorway leading to the stairwell. "How do we find them?"

"Whoa there," said Cal. "No way. We don't know anything about these people. You both stay here with me."

For a moment he reminded Miranda of Pinkie-Sue when she was Being Firm.

Cal turned back to the radio. He'd twisted the loose wires together and was methodically switching one knob after another. Nothing happened until he flicked a switch marked SPEAKER. Then the crackle of radio static filled the room.

"We have some progress, guys," he said, holding

down a red button with his thumb. He spoke into the microphone.

"This is *Oscilla Star*. Mayday. We're north of Cary Bay. Nearing Dummity Beach. Mayday, Mayday. . ."

"I don't know how to help," said Miranda tersely. She hated being told what to do. Surely she should just go and find the crew?

"It's all done by computers, usually," said Cal, not listening. "Only the computers aren't working." He scratched his head. "There must be a sat-phone up here."

"Look." Jackie pointed to a peppering of holes in a number of monitors. "They've been shot."

"Gyro-nav," read Miranda, looking at one broken screen. "Oh dear." She clutched the console as the ship leaned to port.

"Shhh," said Cal. "I've found something." He was looking at another, flickering screen.

"Who votes I should drop the anchor?" said Cal.

"Do it," said Miranda.

Cal looked sheepish. "I don't know how yet."

Miranda tried to think. All the big anchors she had seen worked from a kind of winch. She tried to remember what Mrs Garroway had said – something about an anchor being released but not bedding in.

"How many fathoms do you think we are?" asked Cal.

"Ten, maybe?" Miranda knew the bay shelved away steeply.

"This is one big girl," sighed Cal. "How do I do this?"

"Maybe your mobile would work out here?" suggested Jackie.

"I have no mobile," said Cal. "We came out here in our wetsuits to save you."

"So save me," muttered Jackie. "This is seriously scary."

Cal went back to the radio and tried again. "Mayday, Mayday, *Oscilla Star* Mayday."

"I've got to look for the crew. It's our only hope." Miranda started for the door.

But Cal shook his head and put a finger to his lips.

"Hello? Hello? Sorry, no, the captain isn't here. At least I don't think so." He shot a look at Miranda.

"I GOT THROUGH! DON'T WANDER OFF," he ordered.

Jackie hugged Miranda in relief. Help would be here soon.

"No. We're off Dummity Beach. We're coming up to The Teeth. We think we're dragging a drogue. I guess we're going to bottom out. Listing a little. I think we're taking on water. No engines. How do I. . .? No, I'm just a kid. Callum MacNamara. There were pirates. . ."

Miranda looked out of the window. The sky was definitely getting lighter but the cliffs suddenly seemed very close. Too close. One hundred metres ahead the sea ran in a series of white rushing channels, criss-crossing each other, eventually swirling in a foamy mass. The Teeth! She took another step to the door. Was Cal too late?

Miranda examined a table covered with charts, billowing sea maps and notebooks of figures. What did it all mean? Miranda glanced at the map on the top, and it showed the southern ocean. Maybe this was where the pirates were going to take the ship.

"Dude, I don't know where the bow thrust joystick is. . ." Cal said sounding harassed. "What's the wind speed? Er, it's pretty gnarly out there, but not, like, a massive blow, y'know? We're talking five or six footers at the lip, no more."

"Doesn't this thing have a wheel?" Miranda asked.

"A what?" Jackie was slurping the contents of a bottle of orangeade he'd found on the bridge.

"A ship's wheel? You know, for steering? Doesn't this thing have a rudder?"

"Try down there." Jackie pointed to a ladder underneath the front windows. She couldn't believe she hadn't noticed. There was another level down there, right at the front of the bridge, with a ship's wheel dead centre. It was a smallish round device, very like the steering wheel on a car, and not the big wooden spoked wheel that Miranda had imagined.

"Maybe Cal should look at this if all these computers are broken," Miranda suggested.

"They're not all broken," said Jackie. "Look at this one."

Miranda looked at a small black screen with BALLAST written on it in green print. There was an image of the outline of the ship and there were two tanks drawn in. Both were half coloured in.

"If we're listing, shouldn't we have more ballast?" Miranda knew a little bit about boats.

"For sure I don't know where the manual console is," Cal was saying.

There were two small levers either side of the computer screen, one marked "Left Ballast" and one marked "Right Ballast".

"We could just pull on those," said Jackie longingly. "The ballast tanks would fill with seawater, the ship would become more stable and we'd save the day and get medals from the queen, or even Prince William." His eyes widened. "Or maybe even Barack Obama."

Miranda put her hand over the controls. "NO," she said. "We might sink the ship."

"But we have to do something," said Jackie. "We can't just stand here like lemons. We're going to crash anyway, so we may as well work some of these machines because it might just help."

"I'm going to find the crew," whispered Miranda. "You stay here."

"Exact position? We're heading sideways to the reef. It's well flaky." Cal shook his head. "No, I don't know the coordinates." He raked his fingers through his hair as he studied the machines surrounding him, trying to understand whatever was being told to him on the end of the line.

The ship let out another ear-splitting groan as it spun slowly round, the stern now facing the bay. *Think of the baby seals*, Miranda told herself sternly when the panic threatened to overwhelm her.

"Cal, there's a ship's wheel down there." She pointed at the ladder. "Can't you steer us through the reef and run us aground on to the beach? You know where all the rocks are better than the computer."

"You'd like me to surf a twenty-five-thousand-tonne oil tanker round The Teeth and over a sand rip on to the beach sideways?" pointed out Cal. "I can't steer a ship which has no power. It won't work."

"Try anyway," said Miranda.

"If it works then I guess we might try and turn her, attempt some kind of sick back-hander, say," muttered Cal. He looked at the phone. "Oh no, dude, I wasn't talking to you." He put his hand over the receiver and pointed at Miranda. "The Coastguard dude wants us all on deck with life jackets on. He says it will take about forty-five minutes to scramble a helicopter and maybe twenty to get the lifeboat out here."

"Too long!" Miranda was in the doorway now.

"Which throttle?" Cal was talking into the phone again. "I'm a bit, like, in the wilderness here." He looked utterly miserable.

"He could use a hand," said Jackie.

"Don't touch anything," ordered Miranda, and fled down the stairs before Cal could stop her. She stood in front of the map of the ship, steadying herself on the metal banister. She knew there was a chance there were no crew left on board. Red and the pirates might have taken them with them, or worse. But finding them was the only real chance of saving the ship.

She crept along the corridor and found an area which must have been the crew's mess. It was a long broad room with a red table. Smashed plates of food lay on the floor, and there was a poster of a single palm tree growing out of a sand dune taped to the wall. Miranda slid on a spillage of brown liquid that may or may not have been tea.

Miranda paused as a clanking noise beat through the ship. She felt a sudden chill and her arms erupted in goose pimples under her wetsuit.

Somewhere, deep in the ship, someone was pounding the walls or the floor, or some pipes. Glancing out of a porthole Miranda saw that dawn was breaking and she could see the cliffs clearly. In a few more minutes they would be on the rocks. It was almost too late. Summoning up all her courage, she forced herself to go deeper into the dark, oil-smelling ship. She followed the sound; sometimes it was louder, sometimes more faint. She travelled down four flights of metal staircases and then she found herself in a huge noisy room. Machines lined the walls, big grey boxes, covered in dials and switches. Pipes ran over the floor. This must be the engine room. She found a red clipboard on the floor with numbers scrawled on a grid. Down here the sea boomed and the air was hot and stale. Still the knocking carried on, and now she thought she could hear voices. Yes, she could hear a deep voice, shouting. She was covered with fresh chills. If she had found the crew there was a chance they would be saved. Miranda ran on through a grey corridor and then came to a door.

"Help," called a muffled voice, "help, help."

The door was fastened shut by a large handle. Miranda pulled and tugged, but it wouldn't budge.

"Don't worry, I'll get you out," shouted Miranda,

wondering how she was going to do it. She looked around for something to help. There was a coil of rope hanging on the wall, and a lifebelt. No good. Miranda tried again; she thought of the danger she was in, she thought of Cal losing his mind on the bridge. She thought of Jackie, his hands on a lever, itching to pull. Miranda shoved hard and the handle bit into her palms, but moved a fraction. Miranda shoved again. Nothing. She thought of the ship broken on the rocks, black fluid seeping out the side, clouding in the water, spreading out over the shore and creeping closer and closer to the seals.

The handle suddenly gave and swung up. The door flew open.

Miranda threw her hand over her mouth. This was all wrong. She stared, unable to move, as a thickset man glared back at her.

It was so unlikely, so crazy.

"Mr Babbing?" she stammered.

194

CHAPTER TWENTY-FIVE

Miranda's Swim

Mr Babbing pushed past her and scanned the corridor.

"Who brought you here?" he demanded in a rough voice Miranda had not heard before. She couldn't answer. Her throat had gone dry and all she could do was stare at him.

Mr Babbing eyed her speculatively. "What do you know?" he asked.

"Nothing," gasped Miranda. This was true enough.

Mr Babbing looked back into the room. "All clear," he said. A second person emerged in boots, heavy trousers and a black waterproof coat.

"Hello, Miranda," said Mrs Babbing. "Surprise!"

Miranda tried to think, but her head was whirling. Were the Babbings in league with Red? Were they pirates or police investigators?

She began to back away down the corridor, not knowing who was good and who was bad.

The Babbings were murmuring together. Miranda tripped over a coil of rope and righted herself.

"We're the police," said Mr Babbing. "Come here. You're safe now."

Miranda hesitated. "Have you got any identification?" That was what people said on television.

"Thanks to you, we can sort this out," said Mr Babbing, ignoring the question. He held out his hand. Mrs Babbing seemed angry and muttered something to her husband.

"We're going to crash on The Teeth," said Miranda in a small voice. "It's an emergency." She edged further away. In a few more paces she would reach the corner. Then there was a flight of stairs. But where did she want to go?

"But what will we do with them?" asked Mrs Babbing in a voice that was not quiet enough. Mr Babbing raised his arm to steady himself. His coat fell open and Miranda saw the unmistakable outline of a small gun in a leather shoulder holster.

This was enough for Miranda to turn and run, the adrenalin making her move faster than she had ever done before. Mr Babbing let out a shout and came haring after her. She could hear his feet pounding on the floor. He was almost upon her when he slipped and fell heavily into the wall.

Miranda fled to the stairs, racing down and down, her feet clanging on the treads. And then she was in a low-ceilinged narrow corridor. It was horribly claustrophobic but she raced through it. She guessed she was in the bottom of the ship. Both the Babbings were after her now, breathing hard. The fear was awful, but she kept going. Her plan was to outrun these two, and hide until help came. The thick, stale air made her throat hurt. But the Babbings were running much faster than she thought possible for old, fat people. Miranda splashed over the oily, puddled floor, turned a sharp corner and fled down a dark corridor. She had no idea where she was or where she was going. Miranda fled through an open door into a dimly lit space and eyed circular hatches in the floor. She dashed to the first hatch and twisted the metal handles. Slowly the thing began to move. She twisted it right round and the lid clicked and she was able to pull it open. It was dark inside, and she could hear water sloshing around. The only way down was via a thin metal ladder. Dare she do it?

Miranda climbed into the hole and pulled the lid back. It shut with a dull ring. She clung to the ladder in utter darkness, breathing in fast little pants, more terrified than she had ever been in her life. The ship swayed and deep water sloshed below her. It was airless down here and it smelled putrid. She was fairly sure she was in a ballast tank. She heard footsteps above and held her breath. The footsteps came closer, and Miranda felt a tug on her head as she moved and had the stultifying realization that a lock of her hair was trapped in the hatch. The footsteps stopped overhead and Miranda heard voices. The Babbings were arguing. Had they seen her hair?

She screamed as the hatch was thrown open and hands grabbed her wrists, yanking her painfully out of the hole.

These two were definitely not police officers. Mr Babbing dragged her to her feet. He was ferociously strong. She was propelled out of the big empty room back through the corridors. Her mind was racing through her fear. Did this mean Red was the goody? Was he actually a policeman? Or was he involved too?

"Up," ordered Mr Babbing, and pushed her on to the staircase.

"Ouch!" she yelled. She'd banged her side on the steps. She wriggled round and glared furiously at them. She was hustled up the stairs and when they reached the top of the third flight, Miranda tried to break free.

"HELP!" She screamed and fought madly, kicking and biting as she was dragged along.

Then they were out the blowy foredeck. The air rushed at her and the seabirds wheeled around, screeching.

"If you don't stop it, we will throw you overboard," said Mr Babbing calmly. He grabbed her and held her over the railings, so Miranda could see the sea far below.

"Are you kidnapping me?" gasped Miranda bravely, though it was fairly clear this was the case.

"We're recouping some of our loss," said Mr Babbing in a nasty voice.

"What?"

"You're worth, what, twenty barrels of oil?" snarled Mr Babbing. "You'd better pray your parents have got

198

savings."

Miranda wisely kept her mouth shut.

It was getting much lighter now. The sky was streaked with orange. The Babbings only had to lift Miranda's leg and she would be tipped into the sea.

She heard something else, then, like a roar of voices, and she craned her neck round. Further down the deck, Mrs Babbing was operating a machine which was causing the lifeboat hanging above to grind and squeak, but beyond him there was a small window, and pressed against it were many, many hands.

Here and there Miranda could see the odd boiler-suited cuff.

The crew!

"HELP," she screamed as Mr Babbing pinned her arms behind her back.

She looked as the lifeboat was lowered over the deck, and as it swung near, Mr Babbing picked her up and tossed her inside.

Miranda lay gasping in the scuppers of the boat. It would take maybe twenty people at the most. It was dirty, covered in bird poo. Miranda grabbed the side as the boat swayed through the air. She could not look as the davits lowered her down and down, the boat swinging and creaking horribly. Mr Babbing was next to her, gripping the side of the boat and examining the controls.

"No funny business," he said, and turned his back on her to unhook the chain as the boat landed with a splash in the waves.

Miranda looked over the side. They were a couple of metres from the stern of the *Oscilla Star*. She could see the beach, and there, in darkness, was The Dodo Hotel, its upper windows winking in the dawn light like it was watching her through spectacles. She looked again. There was a tall figure in black, standing on the parapet, gazing out to sea.

Hugo?

Miranda had no time to think about it as the *Oscilla Star* groaned above them and a ladder was lowered into the boat. Mrs Babbing scrambled down. Mr Babbing unhooked the chains and the lifeboat drifted free. He started up the engine and started to turn the boat round.

"Where are we going?" asked Miranda as they bobbed on the waves.

"Be quiet," roared Mr Babbing as the sound of a helicopter in the distance broke the morning air.

"That traitor," spat Mrs Babbing.

"Shut up," warned Mr Babbing, looking back at Miranda.

Miranda pushed herself to the back of the lifeboat. She slowly began loosening her life jacket. Next to them the *Oscilla Star* made a rattling, clanking noise and started to move in a new direction, the bow moving round clockwise. Through her panic, Miranda wondered if Cal had dropped the main anchor.

Mr Babbing pulled back the throttle and turned the boat. Wherever they were headed, it wasn't to the shore. He started to argue furiously with his wife. Miranda deliberately took deep, slow breaths, filling her body with oxygen as she gazed at the beach. It was maybe three hundred metres to shore. What was more dangerous, the sea or the Babbings? At least the tide would pull her in. She undid the clips on her life jacket and lifted it over her head. She put a leg over one side of the boat. Then, in front of the astonished faces of the Babbings, she jumped overboard.

CHAPTER TWENTY-SiX

Cal's Biggest Ride

Miranda dived, fighting the currents that were sweeping her upwards. She swam hard in what she hoped was the direction of Dummity Rock. She saw only shapes and shadows, areas of dark and light. The cold was making her head numb. She heard the rumble of the lifeboat and, glancing up, saw its dark shell directly above her. The propellers churned the water and made it impossible to see anything. Miranda dived deeper and swam on. She didn't need air, not yet. She could cover a greater distance below water than above it. She knew she was in the most dangerous situation of her life. But she didn't need to surface. She could hold her breath for a great deal longer. But as she beat on, inklings of fear crept over her and she had to steel herself not to panic. Something small and black darted in front of her – a seal! Miranda followed in its wake, hoping it was fleeing to safety.

The boat sounded further away. Surely the Babbings would have to leave soon or they'd be spotted by the Coastguard's lifeboat. This must be the longest she had ever held her breath. It was beginning to hurt, but she could cope with that. She could hear her heart thumping and the water rushing around her. She was floating upwards, but she needed to lie safe, in the deep. She battled to get down but a current brought her closer to the surface and she ploughed on through the water. She pictured Pinkie-Sue, her lovely mother. Would she ever see her again?

Her lungs were really protesting now. If she didn't breathe soon she'd be in trouble. Miranda tried to ignore the pain but her head was pounding and she felt dizzy and strange and she knew she had to breathe or risk blacking out. She took a few more strokes but her lungs felt crushed; there was nothing left. Miranda fought to the surface, broke through and drank in the air. Her eyes smarted with salt, but she was within striking distance of Dummity Rock and the Babbings' lifeboat was now maybe fifty metres away. But Mr Babbing had seen her. She trod water, trying to regain her strength. To her horror, Mr Babbing turned the boat and powered it in her direction.

What did he want with her? It wasn't fair! She'd escaped! The cold was pressing her temples and she felt a bottomless fear as the boat got closer and closer.

He was going to run her over. The boat was nearly on her and she dived as something vast moved between them. The roughness of its skin made Miranda shriek underwater and she broke the surface, coughing and spluttering. A wide mouth gaped and shut as a dorsal fin emerged. The basking shark was right here beside her. The Babbings' lifeboat swerved to avoid smashing into the huge creature and rocked to and fro like a toy. The creature floundered in the waves and Miranda heard Mrs Babbing shrieking, "JUST GO."

Giddy with adrenalin, Miranda dived again, making for Dummity Rock and barrelling through the water. The shark had saved her! At last her fingers touched the cold wet rock and she found a foothold with her toes. She pulled herself to the surface and looked cautiously around. Twenty metres away was the fin of the shark, and beyond that, haring away to the west, were the Babbings. Miranda inched her way out of the water, clinging like a reptile to the rock. When she'd reached the flat upper ledge she turned to look at the sea. The Babbings were just a speck on the horizon and now, bombing round the headland, was the *Maurice and Joyce Hardy*, the all-weather orange lifeboat from Fowey. Miranda's heart was beating so wildly it was all she could do to just sit and watch, and wait for her body to calm down. The boat skirted round the *Oscilla Star* and Miranda wondered if her brothers were making their way to the deck. She sat trembling and clinging to the rock. On the other side of the bay the *Oscilla Star* was swinging round. Had Cal really managed to drop a second anchor? The immense ship was now clear of The Teeth and was gliding towards land in the deep water channel, about three hundred metres from the shore. Two hundred metres;

a hundred and fifty metres. It was almost level with her, and so close she could see the barnacles stuck to the side. And there was a massive anchor chain, taut against the sky. All at once a helicopter, a Royal Navy Sea King crashed out of the sky and tailed the Babbings, roaring away over the dawn sea. A second helicopter quickly arrived, and hovered above the tanker as it washed nearer the beach. Everything seemed to switch into slow motion: the helicopter overhead, the arrival of lights of emergency vehicles on the cliffs and the slow movement of the ship itself.

Then it stopped, Miranda guessed only twenty metres offshore, held fast by anchor chains to the bow and stern. All over the bay the seabirds were all going crazy, diving and screeching, swooping round the ship like they were trying to attack it.

Was it going to tip? To crack in two like the *Titanic*? It was utterly shocking to see something as huge as the *Oscilla Star* so close to the shore.

Miranda waited, so stunned she could barely breathe, but the ship didn't move. She sat for a long time until finally she thought it was safe to go. Then she clambered back into the water and swam for the shore, keeping far away from the colossal tanker.

She was so cold now her fingers were turning blue and her teeth were chattering. She crossed the beach and climbed over the rocks and the splintered surfboard to the Seal Cave, where she found her clothes lying in a huddle where she'd left them earlier. She was so stiff that she could hardly pull them on.

She didn't think about anything apart from what she was doing. But when she came out of the cave she saw that the *Oscilla Star* seemed to be swarming with people. The Sea King was positioned above it, and a man was coming down on a rope. The cliffs above her rang with the sound of sirens and a second, smaller lifeboat bobbed in the waves beyond The Teeth. Miranda wondered where Cal and Jackie were but felt sure they were safe now they weren't going to explode on The Teeth.

She sat behind the Whale Stone, washing the bloody scratches on her feet (how had she got them?) in a rock pool. Her teeth were still chattering but she could sense some kind of warmth enveloping her body. And now the sun had come up over the sea, the chill had gone from the air. Miranda teased the seaweed from her hair and wrapped her arms round her knees. She could hear talking coming from The Dodo Hotel, men's voices, and radioed responses. But for now, she just wanted to sit. She felt a cold pressure on her cheek and jumped. Fester stood there, bedraggled and wagging. Miranda put her arms round the dog and hugged him.

"I'm back," she told him.

She saw no reason to show herself. The police and the navy and the Coastguard and whoever else had enough to do without worrying about her, so she just sat. Soon the beach was alive with people. She felt sure someone would find her soon. She pinched herself to make sure she was still alive. She'd maybe wait just a little bit longer. She wondered if she had the energy to walk round the cliffs to find her seals but she was so tired. Fester growled as a couple of gulls landed on the rock next to her and watched her speculatively.

"You can't eat me," said Miranda. They hopped closer and she shot out a foot and scared them off. That hurt. Her whole body ached. No wonder she couldn't move.

Then Fester was growling again.

"Well done," said a voice just by her ear. Miranda shook her head. This wasn't happening. She had made it, the *Oscilla Star* was saved. And now, this! Red was standing right next to her, blocking out the sun. Her chest suddenly felt tight.

"I won't hurt you," said Red. "I'm sorry I was rude to you guys last night." Like the Babbings, he was dressed all in black. He had huge rings under his eyes and his hands were smudged with oil. "What happened out there?"

Miranda wondered whether anyone would hear her if she screamed. There was so much noise surrounding the *Oscilla Star*.

"Are you a policeman?" she asked hopefully.

"Yes and no," replied Red. "I try to stay away from the police." He tickled Fester's head and dog leaned against his legs.

Traitor.

Could she run? Miranda felt so weak she didn't think she could even stand. This was like waking from a nightmare, only to find it was real.

"I'm not a policeman as you know them," he said unhelpfully.

"Special branch? Spy? MI5?" asked Miranda, her fear abating a little. "I saw you leave the ship on a speedboat."

Red watched the activity on the ship. It looked like the remaining crew had been released and were being brought up on the deck. Miranda wanted to go and find her brothers but her legs just wouldn't work.

"None of those. I've been trying to police some people. It's different." He sat next to Miranda on her rock and she curled her lip and edged away.

"I was trying to stop the Babbings. They're major criminals. They've been planning this job for months. They had it all lined up; engineering the deal at Novorossiysk – that's in Russia; bribing half the crew of the *Oscilla Star* before it even left port. They planned to join the ship here, pay off the crew and steal thousands of tonnes of crude oil, and then hide out on the southern oceans. The oil is worth millions and the Babbings have got connections all over the world. The ship was old. Badly managed, it could have caused an environmental catastrophe." He threw a pebble against a rock. "I had to stop those people. They're out of control and think they can do whatever they want."

"Piracy in the English Channel?" said Miranda.

"Pirates are everywhere," replied Red. He shaded his eyes and watched the army helicopter fly overhead.

"What would they have done with the oil?" asked Miranda. "Where were they going to take the ship?"

"Like I said, they've got contacts all over the world, especially in countries that aren't especially friendly with the West."

"So was it you who locked the Babbings away?" asked Miranda.

Red nodded.

"How did you get on board?" asked Miranda.

Red checked his watch. "I have a boat I keep in Belieze Harbour. And the Babbings didn't perceive me as a threat," he said. "Are your brothers on that ship?"

"How do you know all this?" asked Miranda, not answering. She forced herself to her feet. "If you're not a policeman, then who are you?"

Red looked at her. "You haven't guessed?"

"No."

"I'm their son," he said. As Miranda backed away, he held up his hands. "Hey, don't hold it against me. You can't choose your parents."

CHAPTER TWENTY-SEVEN

Goodbye to The Dodo

It was a blowy spring afternoon, the tide was right out, and the sun was sinking towards the ocean. Six months had passed since Cal had saved the *Oscilla Star*. Dummity Bay had been inundated with newspaper journalists, TV reporters, sightseers, Russians, bloggers and ecologists. Oil tanker experts, police detectives, Coastguard staff, military personnel and government investigators had arrived in droves.

The Dodo had been the HQ of the whole operation and for the first time, all of its rooms were full. Now they'd all left. Miranda zipped up her new blue cardigan and ran to join her family on the beach. The MacNamaras were gathered for the first barbecue party of the season. Cormac, soon to be A Published Author, was chatting cheerfully to Doris's mother as Pinkie-Sue swept up and down, dispensing drinks to friends, neighbours and relatives. Since his brief stint as a hotelier last autumn, Jackie had become passionate about cooking and was now bossily manning the barbecue, Fester lying hopefully at his feet. They'd even managed to prise Granny Lamarque out of London, and she sat in a deckchair in brand-new wellies and a green salwar kameez, trying to get a signal on her phone. Granny MacNamara was flirting with a bunch of Cal's surfer friends and Doris was telling Mrs Garroway about Clover. The octopus had grown much too big for her tank and a few months after being moved to the larger aquarium in Newquay, she'd inexplicably laid thousands of eggs.

The *Oscilla Star* was gone. She had been refloated out of the bay on the high tide of the autumn equinox and then piloted to a Portsmouth refinery, where the oil had been safely pumped out. The ship was now apparently anchored offshore of Portugal, waiting for repairs. It was all down to Cal that it hadn't been more badly damaged.

Miranda thought back to the day the *Oscilla Star* had run aground. Cal and Jackie had been searching for Miranda when they'd discovered the anchor release gear to the bow of the ship. Between them they had operated the winch which played out the chain, and eventually managed to anchor the ship – though they admitted they'd let too much chain go before they'd thought to stop it.

After Red had left, Miranda had remained hidden, watching as various lines were attached to the ship by the

211

Royal Navy. An inflatable powerboat kept delivering various equipment on the shore before speeding off again.

Miranda waited as the crew – six men in orange boiler suits and one man in a dark green shirt and trousers, probably the captain – were escorted down the ladder and off the ship. They were taken away in a Royal Navy powerboat.

But where were her brothers?

Only when Jackie and Cal appeared on the portside deck did Miranda and Fester fly out from the Whale Rock and run shrieking over the beach.

"I'M HERE, I'M HERE!"

A man in a reflective jacket and hard hat grabbed her arm. "Are you the missing girl?"

"MIRANDA! BABE!" howled Cal from the deck of the ship. He gave a yelp of joy. "WE THOUGHT YOU'D WIPED OUT! You UBER CHICK! WE'VE BEEN SHEDDING TEARS OVER YOU!"

"I DIDN'T CRY," shouted Jackie, dancing up and down. "IT WAS GRIT IN MY EYES."

Three military-looking men were standing beside them.

"IT WAS THE BABBINGS!" shrieked Miranda. "THEY'RE INSANE!"

"WE LOVE YOU, BETTY!" howled Cal.

"AND I LOVE YOU, FESTER," shouted Jackie.

"NOW CAN YOU TELL THESE DUDES I'M NOT A PIRATE?" called Cal.

The three of them had stayed the night with Doris and her mother. The next morning they'd waited for ages in the hot, stuffy sitting room. Everyone sat on the green velvet three-piece suite. Miranda wore Doris's pyjamas and dressing gown. She had two broken ribs, mild hypothermia and a broken finger. Jackie had a cut on his cheek and bruises on his legs, sustained during his struggle with Mr Babbing. He was fiddling with the sofa tassel and trying to ignore Fester howling in the garden. Cal sat next to Doris. He had dark bruises on his wrists but was in very high spirits. When the naval officers had arrived on the ship, they had taken one look at Cal, with his stubble and his long dripping hair, and had thought he was a pirate. He had been quite roughly handled until he'd managed to convince them otherwise.

Aunty Mad was here too, watching TV. When she'd arrived she'd given each sibling a quick pat, then shaken her head.

"You amaze me," she said, and for the most part had seemed too dazed to add much more.

Yesterday had just been a blur of hospital visits, police interviews and then coming here. The MacNamara children had been questioned by the police again this morning.

Miranda caught Aunty Mad looking at her.

"We thought you'd drowned," she finally blurted.

Miranda remembered sitting on her rock in the sunshine. Everyone said she'd been in shock.

Of course everybody wanted to know all the details about the Babbings, Red and the hijack. Cal thought he mostly understood and had drawn out a flow chart to help. But Aunty Mad didn't seem to get any of it.

"It's a little confusing," she said wearily.

CAL'S FLOW CHART

↓

SHADY BABBINGS SEAL DEAL WITH UBER DODGY CREW IN RUSSIAN PORT DURING LAME TWINNING PROGRAMME.

↓

BABBINGS STAKE OUT DUMMITY BAY AS SITE FOR HIJACK. HIDE WEAPONS AND CASH IN OUR OUTHOUSE.

↓

BABBINGS PLAN TO JOIN *OSCILLA STAR* WITH WONGA. JACKIE BUTTS IN WHILST WEAPONS ARE RETRIEVED, THE GROMS SNAKE HIM AND HE'S TAKEN ABOARD *OSCILLA STAR.*

↓

OSCILLA STAR GETS JACKED. GOOD SAILOR DUDES ARE IMPRISONED. DURING AGGRO, NAVIGATION EQUIPMENT GETS WRECKED.

↓

JACKIE IS SLAMMED UP. USES NOODLE AND TRANSMITS SOS TO SPOOKED ONSHORE FEM.

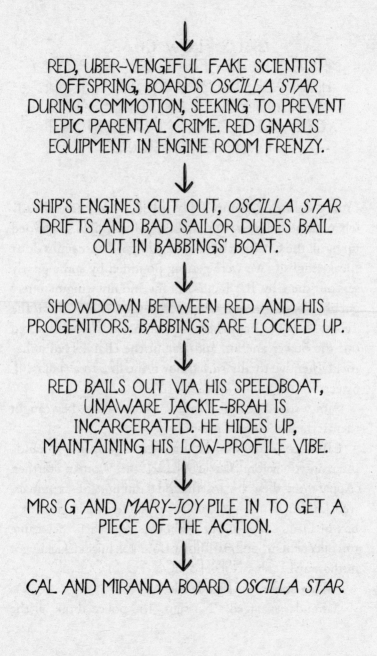

↓

RED, UBER-VENGEFUL FAKE SCIENTIST OFFSPRING, BOARDS *OSCILLA STAR* DURING COMMOTION, SEEKING TO PREVENT EPIC PARENTAL CRIME. RED GNARLS EQUIPMENT IN ENGINE ROOM FRENZY.

↓

SHIP'S ENGINES CUT OUT, *OSCILLA STAR* DRIFTS AND BAD SAILOR DUDES BAIL OUT IN BABBINGS' BOAT.

↓

SHOWDOWN BETWEEN RED AND HIS PROGENITORS. BABBINGS ARE LOCKED UP.

↓

RED BAILS OUT VIA HIS SPEEDBOAT, UNAWARE JACKIE-BRAH IS INCARCERATED. HE HIDES UP, MAINTAINING HIS LOW-PROFILE VIBE.

↓

MRS G AND *MARY-JOY* PILE IN TO GET A PIECE OF THE ACTION.

↓

CAL AND MIRANDA BOARD *OSCILLA STAR*

↓

MRS G SHOOTS OFF TO GET HELP, ONLY HER RADIO IS BRYW. BY THE TIME SHE REACHES FOWEY AND DISEMBARKS, CAL HAS ALREADY MADE CONTACT WITH COASTGUARD.

"You got all that, Aunty?" Cal asked. "You know already what happened next. On the bridge I got, like, so gnarled up by all the Coastguard's nautical lingo. Those brahs don't speak English. We were getting pounded by some gnarly sets out there by The Teeth. But me and my wingman here got the drogue sorted, which, like, spun us out from The Teeth. Then we happened on the anchor room, checked out the bower anchor, and let out the chain. Hydraulics rock! Then we totally surfed down the line to a standstill. Sweet."

Aunty stared at him blankly. "Did you say they caught them? The Babbings, I mean?"

"They got captured heading over to Roscoff," Miranda interrupted before Cal confused the woman further. "Apparently they are international millionaire criminals, well known to the police. They'd hidden their guns in a box of Dad's socks in our outhouse. But when they came to collect them, by boat, just before the hijack, Jackie got in the way."

"What about this Red character?"

Miranda shrugged. "No sign. The police think all the

216

electronic stuff in the caves belonged to him. He used it to track his parents and the *Oscilla Star*, but it's gone now."

A car drew up outside and stopped, and everyone tensed.

"They're here." Doris's mum came in, drying her hands on a tea towel. "I'll let them in, shall I?" But Jackie was already running out of the room.

"MUM," he yelled. "MUM."

Then there were sounds; the smooth opening of the door, the brushing of feet on the doormat, the soft thud of a hug and a sniff of tears. There was the hiss and pop of kisses, a deep Irish sigh, a motherly tongue click and the sharp intake of breath required for lifting a sturdy ten-year-old boy into the air and twirling him round.

"So good to see you," sobbed Pinkie-Sue.

Miranda looked at her lap, and examined her chewed nails. So far, no shouting. This was a good sign. Then she could bear it no longer and got up and flew out into the hallway. Cal followed.

The first thing she thought was how old her parents looked, like they'd been away for ten years rather than a week. Pinkie-Sue looked puffy-faced and grey. Cormac had a deep mesh of lines between his eyes and around his mouth. Miranda stood, unable to move. She felt like she was in the bottom of the mermaid aquarium, with all the water pressing down on her.

"Oh my darling," gasped Pinkie-Sue, pulling Miranda near and enveloping her in her big yellow coat. "Oh my wicked, precious, deceitful, clever, brave, lying daughter."

*

217

And now, back on the beach, everything was about to change once more. Miranda took Mrs Garroway aside.

"You know, I never asked how you knew to come out and save us."

Mrs Garroway snorted. "Your Hugo, walking the cliff above my house. We all know he does that if there's going to be a drowning. Last time I saw him walk, it was my own husband got taken."

"Hugo, really?" breathed Miranda.

"I saw him and I thought to myself, dear me, Sophia, I bet those stupid kids are after their deaths."

"*Meur ras*, Mrs G," said Miranda. She turned to look at The Circus. "Thank you too, Hugo."

Though of course she did not believe in him.

Cal arrived on the beach. He was wearing new board shorts and a billowing blue shirt. He went up to Cormac and slapped him on the back.

"Are you sad, big kahuna?"

"A little," admitted Cormac, straightening his tie. "Are you?"

"Nope," said Cal.

"You look great," Cormac told his son. "Have you been spending your fortune?"

Cal smiled. Soon after the adventure with the *Oscilla Star*, Cal was given a hundred and fifty thousand pounds' reward money from the ship's owners, for saving the ship and its oil. They were so pleased with him they'd invited the whole family to come for a luxury holiday on the Black Sea. It was the stuff of dreams.

218

Cal had decided very quickly what he wanted to do with the money. Eight hundred pounds had gone into Miranda's car fund, and £3.99 had bought Jackie the biggest chocolate bar in the garage. Both children were ecstatic.

The rest of the money, Cal had invested in property. And now, at the age of seventeen, he had become the co-owner of The Dodo Hotel. This had, of course, paid off the debts and enabled them all to stay, something that made everyone very happy. But now Cal wanted a change. He tapped his glass and waited until everyone fell silent.

"People, family, dudes and hot babelinis." He winked at Doris. "It is time for us to move on from the disasters of the past." Cormac winced at this, but Pinkie-Sue squeezed his hand and whispered the title of his book in his ear. "No business can expect to rock with a name like The Dodo. My dear parents renamed this hotel as a nod to our mother's Mauritian vibe. And totally no disrespect, but the dodo is an extinct bird, right?"

"Right," agreed everyone.

"So it gives me great pleasure to rename this old shack. . ." Pinkie-Sue squeezed Cormac's hand again.

"The Precious Pearl Hotel."

THE END

© Daniel Loumeau   www.lumo.co.za

Acknowledgements

Thanks to my fabulous editor, Marion Lloyd, for steadfast support and guidance over the years.

Thanks to Geoff Matthews and his team at HM Coastguard for advice and for answering my crazy questions. I apologise for the dreadful liberties taken in nautical matters.

Especial thanks to Sarah Turner for her story about the sleeping baby seal.

Thanks to Dan.

I must also credit Maeve for supplying the perfect new name for The Dodo, and also Wilfred – my Cornish research assistant, and Arthur – deadline enforcement officer.

Glossary

SURFING GLOSSARY

Aloha: Hello/goodbye

Amped: Charged up

Axed: Being hit by wave

Babelini: An attractive female

Bail out: To jump off board to avoid wipe out

Boardies: Surfing shorts

Brain Freeze: When your head hurts from the cold
water

Brudah/brah/bruh: Brother or close friend

Dude: A person

Gnarly: Rough, bad weather. Or it can mean very good!

Goofyfoot: Putting left foot forward on surf board

Grey-Belly: Older surfer

Hanging Ten: Standing on surf board with ten toes draped
over edges

Kahuna: Coolest dude on the beach

Sick: Extremely good

Wipeout: Fall off board and get smashed by wave

Note: all of the above are subject to varying interpretations.

CORNISH GLOSSARY

Badna Mouy tay: A drop more tea
Comero Weeth: Take care
D aa lowar o ve: I'm OK
Darzona: God Bless
Deeth Da: Good day
Fat La Genes?: How are you?
Gocky/Gokki: Foolish, stupid
Metten Daa: Good morning
Meur Ras: Thank you
Pynjay: Parrot
Tabm mouy bara: A bit more bread please